Finding
SINCLAIR

Finding
SINCLAIR

Book 2 of the Sinclair Series

DENISE JAXON
Story Goddess Publishing
www.storygoddesspublishing.com

Copyright © 2022 Denise Jaxon
ISBN: 979-8-9863000-0-9 (paperback)

Story Goddess Publishing
www.storygoddesspublishing.com

DEDICATION

This book is dedicated to
Alice and Dennis

PROLOGUE

The Least of These
We never know what will be, so we plan so endlessly
what we think is not to be, is really our true destiny.
We search for the why of everything, not trusting in what's unseen,
trying to control our hand, when the dealer is in command.

Remember the least of these, it's a call to you and me,
it's the path life will take us down
where our souls will be found

Life will throw us a curve ball, but save someone else from their fall,
cause things don't always go in our favor, but our blessings will
come later.
There's a reason why we're here, just listen it will be revealed.
Peace will come, when our work is finally done.

Remember the least of these, it's a call to you and me,
it's the path life will take us down
where our souls will be found

CHAPTER 1

C hicago sings in the summertime. It's a melody of south side harmony, against the baseline of the Magnificent Mile, the hook of the Loop and the chorus of Grant Park, where I was headed for the sixth annual Taste of Chicago. The winter had finally taken a seat so that the vibrant days of summer could take center stage, and there was no better audience than the 4th of July's Taste of Chicago.

I eased my car through traffic, softly cursing myself for not taking Danny's advice and catching the L instead. Even though we had VIP parking, getting to the designated spot meant facing the dogged gridlocked streets surrounding the festival. I checked my watch and sighed—I was going to be late. Danny and I had agreed to meet at Buckingham Fountain since he would be working and already near the Loop. A situation that was annoying in itself, and the added traffic nightmare only exacerbated that fact. Danny's career had taken off after he worked the insider trading case that landed Tony in jail. His reward—more high-profile cases, which resulted in less time for us to spend together. We were planning our wedding, and it was quickly falling on me while he focused on his rising career.

I finally made my way to the parking location and jetted from my car, practically jogging toward Buckingham Fountain. I zigzagged between the hundreds of people who had converged on the area to enjoy food, music and the dynamic environment that was the heart of this city by the lake. I saw Danny in the distance and was calmed by his million-dollar smile. The woman standing next to him caught my eye, and I held my smile even though inside, it had flatlined when I recognized who she was.

"Hi, babe," Danny said, grabbing me around my waist and planting a kiss on my lips. "I have a surprise for you." He turned toward the woman standing next to him and put his other arm around her waist. "Meet my mom, Carla Boone, Esquire," he said, tipping an imaginary hat and bowing toward her. "I thought it would be great if she came and helped you with the wedding plans."

I held my plastered smile. "How thoughtful of you," I managed to say behind my façade. I knew his mother was an attorney but wondered if introducing her as "Esquire" was some kind of joke. I reached out to shake her hand, wishing Danny would have prepared me for this blindsided surprise. I mean, honestly, surprising me with a visit from his mother! I stood there, my hand dangling in mid-air for what felt like an eternity.

Instead, Carla threw her arms around me. "I'm so glad to finally meet you, Sinclair. You're more beautiful than Daniel described."

I was surprised at how easily I relaxed into her arms. Her presence was powerful and inviting at the same time, not the unapproachable woman I had imagined with all of her accomplishments and status. Danny always talked about the odds she'd overcome to get where she was and how she raised him with no tolerance for mediocracy. I concluded any woman with all of her attributes would be a hardcore bitch, who didn't suffer fools lightly.

We released our hug and she held me at arms-length. Her

light brown eyes sparkled against her coffee-with-a-hint-of-cream complexion, complimented by the brown highlights that streaked through curly ringlets that framed her girlish round face. I could see why Trace never stopped loving her. Danny hadn't told her about my relationship with Trace, and at this moment, I was glad he hadn't. In spite of all of the confidence I possessed, next to her, I felt like the rebound girl.

"Daniel tells me you may appreciate a little help planning the wedding," she said. Her voice void of any future mother-in-law judgment.

"It's just that he's been so busy; well, we're both really busy, but it's harder for him to get away so we can—"

"Of course, you're busy, too. Men!" she said, giving Danny a playful side-eye. "We must not let them think that their work is more important than ours." She gazed at me with a look that warmed me from the inside out. Her gift of making one feel like you're the most important person to her at that moment, had me caught up in her spell. "Speaking of work, Danny tells me you have a mean business sense, and I can't wait to hear all about it," she cradled her arms, and Danny and I linked ours through either side on cue. "Now, let's go. I've been dying to see what all this Taste of Chicago hoopla is about."

We strolled through Grant Park lit up with music stages, vendor and restaurant booths, bar areas for grown folks, and play areas for children. People from all over the city emerged onto Grant Park, Chicago's front yard. It was one of the times this racially separated city came together. From Cicero to Hyde Park to Oaklawn, it seemed the restrictive covenants were swept away for at least a day. At least until we found a place in the food court to eat at a communal table near a white family. The mother smiled sweetly while not so discreetly shifting her purse out of reach when we sat down.

"There it is. Living proof that I am back in the Mid-west." Carla said, gesturing toward the white family.

"Not much has changed there," I said, mocking the woman with an exaggerated gesture when placing my purse down. Now she knows how it feels, I thought as she gathered up her low-rent family.

Carla pointed a bright red painted fingernail at the Cicero clan as they stalked away, "That's why I moved to D.C. We ain't having none of that in the Chocolate City. White folks come in from Virginia and Maryland, know they place."

"It's a wonder Mayor Washington even got into office given the racial divide of this city," Danny said.

"That's cause we got out the vote. There were more new voters registered during Harold Washington's campaign than had been in decades," I added.

I could feel Carla staring at me. "You've got a smart one here, Daniel," she said, that bright red fingernail pointing my way.

"Tell me something, I don't know," he said, blowing me a kiss across the table. "I feel like my head is going to explode when she talks about the stock market and her big real estate deals. She's wheeling and dealing for sure."

"If you can call it that," I said, picking up a rib and sliding the meat off the bone with my teeth. "That's why I ran late today. I'd gone to the final walk-through of the apartment building I'm buying. Property was supposed to be delivered empty, but there's a tenant refusing to move."

"Sounds like a reason to delay escrow, if you ask me," Carla said.

"My agent suggested that, but that proposes other problems. Any more delay and that jeopardizes the deal I put in place to flip the property. I picked it up on foreclosure with a decent amount of equity, and flipping it will bring a hefty profit."

"You'll work it out, baby. Let me know if I need to throw some of my legalize at them; that always gets people in step," Danny said.

"Touché!" Carla had ordered the ribs too, and the poised, proper women I'd been introduced to just hours ago gave way to her south side Chicago roots. She sucked the BBQ sauce from her fingertips. "So, tell me about these stock picks of yours, Sinclair."

"Not doing much stock picking nowadays," I said, sipping my Michelob. "Using my earnings from it to conquer this real estate game. After dealing with Tony and barely escaping a cell block address, I decided my stock market days are over for now."

"Yes, Daniel told me about that. This Tony sounds like a real character. Looks like you dodged a bullet on that one," she said, that red-painted pinky finger pointing my way as she nibbled on another rib.

It had been a year since the trial that landed Tony in federal prison for insider trading. The preacher's kid that I went on dates to church with and thought I was falling in love with, who introduced me to the volatile, but exciting world of playing the market, now sat behind bars serving out a ten-year sentence. He sat in the courtroom, frail from the weight of the charges against him, offering no defense. He was defeated before the jury returned the verdict and offered only an expressionless gaze when the bailiff led him away.

Danny worked the case as an intern working for the federal prosecutor of Illinois, and though he shared very little with me, he did make a point to let me know that I should keep my mouth shut about Tony and our relationship. He'd turned my file over to a junior analyst just before the indictment, so no evidence of my transactions came out in the trial. Danny and I kept our distance during the trial to avoid any conflict of interest. I went incognito to the sentencing; Tony was my friend, after all. He had ghosted me in the end, and after learning of the charges against him, I realized that he wanted to protect me from what he, for whatever reason, had decided to do.

I sat in the back of the courtroom, stunned by the frail man that stood before the judge, the muscles I once lusted over replaced by an emaciated replica of the man I'd placed so high on a pedestal that his fall broke him into pieces with no hope of putting him back together again.

Danny did a good job of steering Carla away from the topic of Tony. We walked through the vendor booths, danced to the music, and ate way too much. Carla's easy smile and infectious laughter continued to remove any uneasiness I felt about her sudden visit. As Danny stood in line to get more beers, Carla and I found seats near the Jazz stage. She pulled out a pack of Benson and Hedges, tapping it gently on her long-manicured finger shaking one out for herself, then offering me one.

"One of the many vices I've managed to avoid," I said.

"It's a bad habit picked up during hours of studying in college. I could go for hours on coffee and cigarettes," she said, flicking her Bic and inhaling the fire before letting the smoke escape.

We sat there in silence for a moment. She was everything Danny had said she was, and I suddenly felt relieved that she would be there to help me plan Danny's and my big day.

CHAPTER 2

J asmine opened her eyes and pulled the covers over her head to block the afternoon sun that beamed through her windows. She pressed her eyes shut and squeezed her forehead as if that would settle the massive pounding in her head. Something next to her shifted in the bed, and she froze for a moment, trying to remember. Things were kind of fuzzy, as they often were when she had too much to drink. She snatched the covers off, revealing a naked body next to her, his delicious muscles creating a tingle between her thighs.

"What the…" She looked over at the ripped chest when the clock on the bedside table caught her eye. "Oh shit!" She shoved the body next to her, "I gotta go. Get up. It's late. Damn," she said, running around the room, gathering up his things.

The head belonging to the muscles opened his eyes, stretching his bulging quads. His erection stood at attention, straight and long, like a pine tree in the forest. Jasmine, moistening her lips, was tempted until—

"Hey! What up, Julie," he said.

"It's Jasmine!" she said, throwing his pants at him.

"Brian," he said.

"Whatever. Get up," she said, tossing him his shirt. "I have to go."

Brian gyrated his hips, "And waste all of this," he said with a wide grin.

Had she not noticed the missing tooth at the club? He slid his tongue in and out through the gap. Was that the secret to his skilled performance? She really didn't have to look him in the face for that... but she was late for class. She glanced over at the clock, then back at the pine tree in the forest. What the hell.

Jasmine crawled across the bed on all fours. Brian flipped her on her back and straddled her; she pressed her legs together. "I'm not ready yet," she said in her sultry voice.

He took the cue, and she was certain the missing tooth played a part in how his tongue easily found the spot that sent her reeling, forgetting that she was going to be late to class, again.

Jasmine slid into her seat in class and joined her cohort mid-discussion, chiming in with the answer to the quantifiable metrics. She had always been that girl, the one who always raised her hand, who always had the answer to the questions. It all came easy to her. Studying was something she could literally do in her sleep. She only needed to read the material once or twice and then visualize it as she slept, forever committing it to her memory, a memory that seemed to place her on the spectrum, though she possessed no other symptoms except that she could tell you the exact time and date that an event occurred in her life or in history. She had a mind like an IBM computer, but her family didn't believe in labels and ignored her elementary school teachers, who tried to tag her with one. 'We believe Jasmine is slight autistic,' they had told her parents. Then that means she's mostly not, and that was the last they would hear of that. Jasmine plowed through her education, often taking her smarts for granted, deciding four years after receiving her undergrad degree in Political Science that she'd better go for her MBA. She was working in sales, and liked planning her own schedule and working from home, but dealing with bosses with the level of knowledge she held in her pinky toe was getting old. She needed to be her own boss, and an MBA was a step in that direction.

The professor droned on with his lecture, but being talked at for long periods was not her learning language. Her mind drifted, clicking from one thought to another, the professor's voice becoming white background noise. Her attention span would slip in and out, only catching a few points. She was a reader and a visual learner. Later she'd read the material and visit the library for more books on the subject until she knew it inside out.

For now, she'd go into her head, rewriting past conversations, constructing what she should have said. She'd rearrange her living room furniture finding the perfect place for everything. She thought about where she might want to hang out tonight, visualizing herself having just two drinks—her limit—but she always managed to drink more, tossing caution to the wind and convincing herself she would stay in control this time.

The shift in the professor's tone brought her back to the room. "Two more weeks left in the summer semester. Your finals will be verbal presentations. As business leaders, you'll be presenting often in your careers, so it will be a real-life experience," the professor said.

Completing the program early caught Jasmine's attention. She jumped on the opportunity to take the summer classes, which were much easier than the semesters she'd just completed in her first year. She spent hours writing and rewriting papers, but the verbal presentation offered for the summer semester was a breath of fresh air and a task she could nail without trying very hard. After all, it was summer and she had parties, concerts and nightclubs to attend.

Jasmine made a beeline for the door once the class was dismissed. She had nothing in common with her cohorts, and making small talk with them zapped her of her energy. The one time she did get caught up in a conversation, it turned to her hair, which she wore in cornrows. Her white cohort commented about how she liked that she wore her hair like Bo Derek's. Jasmine jumped on the opportunity to tell her the history of black women and cornrows, right down to them being used as maps to escape slavery. It was summer and the traditional hairstyle for black women, and the last thing she wanted to spend her time doing was giving white folks black history lessons.

The heels of her shoes tapped against the hardwood floor as she marched down the hallway and out into the summer heat. Chicago was in the midst of a heatwave, another reason for cornrows in the summer, the humidity murdered press and curls, and the natural hairdo was a lifesaver. She noticed looks when she called on some of her clients. They looked at her head instead of into her eyes, as if they were sending a subliminal message about her hair being inappropriate. Some companies had gone as far as setting policies that discriminated against black employees' natural hairstyles. Part of Jasmine's reason for braiding hers was to dare her company to say something.

"Honestly, it's 1986; enough about my hair already." She'd told her cousin, Sinclair. "It's only inappropriate because they hadn't figured out how Bo did it yet. I heard they used glue to keep the braids from slipping loose."

She hopped in her car and cranked it on. She really needed

a new automobile, but this was of sentimental value. Her parents had bought the used Dotson for her when she went away to college. They weren't a well-to-do family, and she knew the sacrifices they had to make to get that car for her. She would drive it until the wheels fell off to honor her parents. Her Dad checked on her from time to time, cautioning her to change the oil regularly and get a tune-up. 'It'll run well over a hundred thousand miles if you take care of it,' he would tell her. He had even taught her how to change the oil herself, which she did, and conquered, a few times while in college when money was tight, but she had a good job now with great pay that even allowed her to send money to her family back in Gary, Indiana every month, even though her parents told her she didn't need to do that. When growing up, they had made so many sacrifices for her and her brother, Kyle, and she wanted to help however she could. Buying a car now just seemed extravagant to her, and Kyle was in no position to help out at home, not from the jail cell that appeared to be a revolving door for him since quitting college.

Jasmine punched in the car lighter and pulled a half-smoked joint from her ashtray, placing the red ambers of the lighter to her joint and sucking in the smoke. She held it in before letting it escape slowly through her lips and letting the effect pour over her before putting the car in drive. She was meeting Sinclair for the happy hour skate on the north side, and she always skated better when she was high.

CHAPTER 3

I watched Carla as she drew the perfect calligraphy letters on the wedding invitations. She had volunteered to handwrite all two-hundred and fifty invitations. The calligraphy was impeccable and softened the edge I was feeling after she persisted that we chose the gold embossed invitations instead of the heart red trim I had chosen. I was always partial to red, and Danny was pleased with the selection at first until his mother made a case about the gold being more sophisticated and he flipped the script quicker than a Chicago Alderman. I acquiesced, feeling double teamed, but convinced myself that it was a minor detail not worthy of debate. After all, his mother had even used her clout and pulled strings to book the singer we wanted for the reception, even though he'd previously told us he was booked on our wedding day.

We had chosen a Valentine's Day wedding, hence the red heart invitations, and while it was just mid-summer, there was so much to do, and I was already anxious that I wouldn't get it all done. Carla had flown back and forth since the Taste of Chicago, helping with the plans. Without her help, I would have been miles behind schedule. So, picking my battles was important; after all, Danny was her only son.

I watched Carla as she sat at my dining room table, concentrating on the detail of every swirl and loop in the letters that were formed by the gold ink pen she used. Danny and I had discussed it but decided not to move in together until after we were married, so Carla was at my apartment a lot during our planning sessions. As she sat there today, in the same spot that Trace had sat just a few years ago, I tried to imagine them together as high school sweethearts. She with her uppity self-righteous demeanor and his laid-back bad boy charm.

I was still flabbergasted that I'd met and was about to marry Trace's son. I wondered how she would respond if she knew that I'd been with a man twenty years my senior, a possible younger version of herself, the same man who knocked her up in high school, making her pregnant with Danny. She looked over at me. "I wish I could write like that," I said, filling the air with useless chatter, afraid that she could read my thoughts about the man whose love we both shared.

"Just something I picked up to settle my mind when working big cases," she said, "It keeps me sane."

That word sane conjured memories of my mother, who spent the better part of my childhood in and out of mental institutions. "So, Danny should brace himself, huh?" I said, coming back to the present.

"He'll need more than a hobby to stay sane when he runs for office. He's going to need a good strong woman by his side." She said this with ease as if it was a done deal that Danny was running for office. He'd made some casual mention about it when he was an intern, but we hadn't had a serious conversation about it. I placed the twenty-two-cent stamp on the completed invitations. Stamps were going up, and I was glad to get my invitations out before Reaganomics dug deeper into our pockets. "We don't have to worry about that; that's not in his near future, anyway," I said, licking another stamp.

The look she gave me made me want to slide into the seat cushions, sink into a black hole and hide from her piercing, judgmental eyes.

Carla morphed into a smirk. "Yes, don't you worry about that, dear," she said, in a tone that made my skin to crawl.

Still shaken by Carla's response, I climbed into Jasmine's car, choking on the weed smoke. "Damn, Jas, It's like Cheek and Chong in here."

She hit the joint, passing it to me, but I waved it away.

She looked at me sideways.

"Carla," I said, needing no further explanation. Jasmine had met Carla and wasn't impressed.

"I'll hold my, told you so," Jasmine said, wheeling the car onto the Dan Ryan. "For now, anyway. Cause that shit show is just getting started."

I ignored the knot in the pit of my stomach. "I'm sure it's nothing. Just the overall stress of wedding planning."

Jasmine patted my knee, "I'm sure," she said, the non-verbal, told you so, loud and clear.

I was hoping skate night would take my mind off the wedding planning blues. We'd been skating since we were kids growing up in Gary, and whenever I got the chance to skate, flying around the rink to the beat of the music, I was in a different world. I was good at it and looked good doing it, and it made me feel good knowing I could do something with such ease that the majority of the world couldn't do at all. I was bullied as a kid and spent a lot of time at home around family, skating with Jasmine and Kyle. Uncle Ervin had covered the backyard with asphalt, where we learned how to skate and how to fall. I hit that asphalt many a day, but crashing was a part of learning until, eventually, having wheels on my feet became second nature. A skating rink opened up while we were in middle school, and I suddenly became the popular girl. Boys liked me because I could skate so well, and girls wanted me to teach them how to do it, which I was happy to do, if it meant they'd stop teasing me and just let me be me.

I laced up my skates, taking time to get the laces just right. The rink was packed, and though I was a superstar skater in Gary, I didn't stand out much in Chicago because everybody could throw down on the rink.

I rolled onto the hardwood, looking good in my midriff top and jeans, eased up alongside my friend Tina and synced in step with Chicago's signature *crazy leg* move on the rink.

"Where's Jasmine," Tina yelled over the music as we hit the curb and maneuvered into a backward skate.

"Getting a cocktail at the bar," I yelled back.

Tina shook her head. "I don't know how that girl drink and skate like that."

"It ain't no thing," I said. We've been skating so long we can do it in our sleep."

"And two sheets to the wind, apparently," Tina said, as the music slowed down and we rolled off the rink into the bullpen area.

Chicago's Happy Hour skate had become the place to be on Friday nights. If you couldn't skate, you could still get your groove on at the bar, pool tables or Pacman tournaments.

We caught up with Jasmine sitting at a table drinking wine and talking to a guy with a toothpick resting on the side of his mouth. He didn't look like he was from Chicago; something about his swagger gave him away. She was telling him that she'd just left class and was looking forward to getting her skate on.

"Class?" He said.

"Yes, getting my MBA."

"What's going on, Jasmine?" Tina said, interrupting their flow.

"So, I got me a businesswoman on my hands," he said, smiling at her.

I couldn't believe I was witnessing Jasmine blush. She was usually curiously cautious with men. She'd been burned so many times that she'd convinced herself that men were on earth for two things, climaxes and making babies when the time came. Otherwise, they couldn't be trusted no further than she could pick one up and throw him. But this guy, I could tell, struck her in a different way. I wanted to give her some space.

"Challenge you to Pac Man," I said to Tina, giving her a hint to stop blocking.

"Girl, I don't want play no damn Pac Man," Tina said, in her Tina way. She looked at the man that had Jasmine on lock "Hi. I'm Tina. What's your name?"

He swished the toothpick around in his mouth. His smile remained constant, but his body language shifted just slightly enough to give me pause.

"They call me Doc. Who you?"

Jasmine answered before Tina could, introducing Doc to both of us. I wanted to ask his real name, the name his mama gave him, but stopped myself. Besides, he dismissed Tina and me with a swiftness and planted his attention squarely back on Jasmine. I watched him reel her in with his attentiveness and compliments. Her eyes sparkled when he talked to her, and she was clearly soaking up all of his attention. I wanted to be happy for her, but something swept over me, like watching a scary movie play out—that suspense of incoming doom.

It wouldn't be the first time I felt this way and then experienced what I felt play out in real life. My Grandmama Pearl used to say I had the gift. That God choose to reveal things to me and I'd one day learn how to receive it. I hadn't made it there yet. I didn't know what to do with these feelings. Sometimes they were as simple as thinking about someone and they would call, or a sense of déjà vu, like I'd already witnessed a scene that was unfolding before me. Or how I felt when Trace disappeared, and even though that was a part of his lifestyle, I knew something was wrong—and it was. He had disappeared because he had been killed.

Jasmine was dealing with a lot. The last thing she needed was some joker playing games with her. They'd rolled onto the floor during the couple's skate. This Doc character didn't even skate like he was from Chicago. Good thing my fiancé worked for the feds, making finding out who he was an easy task.

CHAPTER 4

T ina stepped back to admire the painting she'd hung on the wall. It was an apartment warming gift from Sinclair. She lifted one end to straighten it, then stepped back, eyeballing the adjustment, satisfied that she had picked the perfect place. Standing in the middle of the room, hands on her hips, she scanned the boxes stacked around her. Settling on one with *kitchen items* scrawled across it in black magic marker, she popped it open, unwrapping wads of newspaper from each item and locating the perfect resting place for them in her new spot.

The apartment she found wasn't in the upscale part of Hyde Park where she wanted to live but was still a welcomed improvement over the Cabrini Green project unit she shared with her father and three brothers whenever one of her brothers wasn't locked up. It took forever to save enough money to move out after one of her brothers stole the savings she had tucked in a hiding place in the concrete walls of the housing project she grew up in. She started depositing her money into a bank after that. She was raised in a money order family. Money orders were purchased to pay the rent, the utilities and the cheap rent to own furniture that she figured they had paid for a million times over. She didn't know anything about banks or credit cards or writing checks. Not until she and Sinclair became friends.

Tina turned the radio up and danced along to the tunes that filled her new apartment. The hardwood floors squeaked under her feet, and she had to pry the paint-sealed windows open with a screwdriver, but being in her own place was heaven compared to the rat and roach-infested walls of Cabrini-Green. Her childhood memories were cluttered with trash piled fifteen stories deep in clogged trash chutes, and children rushed to emergency rooms from rat bites. Their rat feasted bodies and threats of tenant protest the incentive that forced Chicago Housing Authority to perform just enough maintenance to kill a few rats and scatter the roaches deeper into the walls. Until the poison wore off and they would reclaim their turf, terrorizing the tenants that existed there.

Tina was finally turning things around. She was a long way from sleeping under the L where she found herself less than two years ago, where the merciless Chicago winter cut through her body like daggers. Sometimes she could still feel the hot throbbing sensation of her frost-bit fingers from countless hours in the sub-zero temperatures that wrapped the windy city in a cocoon from September to May. When she was hired to work at Kahn Telecommunications, Chicago's new cable TV franchise, she began to claw herself out of the whirlpool of destruction she'd been caught up in since being evicted from her first apartment. The scars of being in the streets had keloid in her memory, leaving the constant reminder of the incident that made her swallow her pride and go back home to her father in Cabrini Green. She covered it with the salve of a new job and the promise it brought, reveling instead in the hope she felt when her dad's childhood friend threw her a lifeline and offered her a job as a cable TV installer at Khan.

At first, threatened and a bit jealous of her coworker, Sinclair;

still, they had managed to find the strength in one another that filled a void in themselves and had formed a friendship that bonded over a mutual respect for the other's struggle. Tina was motivated by Sinclair's tenacity and knowledge of things she was never exposed to. She learned quickly that having Sinclair as a friend far outweighed keeping her as an enemy. From showing her how to open a bank account to enrolling in junior college, Sinclair had become her ride or die.

Over her music, Tina heard the piercing sound of the ringing phone. "Hello," she said, secretly hoping it was *him* calling. He said he'd try to get away and come see her tonight.

Instead, a robotic voice on the other end replied, *"You have a call from an inmate at the Illinois Department of Corrections. Press one to accept the call or two to disconnect and block all future calls from this institution."*

Tina breathed in deep, slowly pursing the air from her lips as she let her mind conjure a positive image to push away the dreed the phone call brought over her. Her dad must have given her brother the number. She didn't know which brother it was; it didn't matter. If they were calling her, it meant only one thing, they wanted something. They always wanted something. She had looked up to them growing up. Her father and brothers were all she had left in a world where her mother left one day and never came back, but the bowels of Cabrini Green quickly covered them in the muck of gang, drugs and crime, claiming them for itself.

She looked at the touchpad on her phone as the robotic voice repeated its message. She sat down on top of a box, trying to calm the pounding in her chest and ease the knot in her gut at the thought of her brothers locked in cages subjected to treatment not unlike that of their enslaved ancestors, except that the brutality heaped upon them came just as much from fellow inmates as from the establishment that incarcerated them. Any hope of a real life, even after release, remained locked in the Jim Crow rules that would forever govern over them.

A memory of her first prison visit with one of her brothers flashed before her. The smell of stale cigarettes mixed with the knock-off Pine-Sol swept through her nostrils. The youngest of her brothers emerged through the iron gate, his once muscular frame now just skin that hung on his bones like a man decades his senior. She tracked his distorted walk as he made his way to where she was sitting. Tears streaked her face when he looked at her and lowered his head. His shameful expression was forever a reminder that he would never be the gentle brother she knew before the prison walls became his home.

Reluctantly, not being able to turn her back on family, she pressed one on the phone. "Who this?" she said into the handset.

He started out with chit-chat at first. She was fine, how was he, blah, blah, blah. Then the ask came, could she send him some money? Why was he in prison this time, she asked. Something he didn't do, was always the answer. Her brothers got locked up for stuff they didn't do more than anyone she knew. After years of re-cidivism, they seemed to thrive in prison, where on the outside, they floundered, even appeared miserable. She knew a prison record for a black man on the outside was no crystal stairs, but wondered how being inside prison walls trumped freedom. She agreed to send him what he asked for and ended the call with, I love you, and she meant that.

She put away her kitchen items and drew a bath. She wanted to put her brother out of her mind. She worried about how they wore on their father and rested easy in the fact that they came to her instead of sucking dry the little life their dad had left. He was only fifty-six, but life had worn him down. After her mother took off, he was never the same. He worked two jobs to keep their low rent lives together, leaving the impressionable minds of young boys to the streets of south Chicago to raise. Tina tried to replace her mother, making sure that food was cooked and the house was clean, but it was no easy feat at ten years old, struggling to be the adult among three growing boys. She watched her father bury his hurt in a bottle of cheap vodka and how the booze lulled him into a mere frame of a man, existing in a world where the odds were stacked against him, and the bets placed him on the losing end of every hand.

Tina had buried the abandonment by her mother somewhere between her anger and her low self-esteem. It was a matter she thought she had under control. Still, the effects were simmering just under the surface and revealed itself in ways she wouldn't understand for years to come.

The phone rang again, and this time it was *him*. He would be there shortly. She adjusted her schedule whenever he called, placing his needs and time before her own. She finished her bath and rubbed her wet skin from head to toe with cocoa butter. He said he liked the way it smelled and how it made her skin soft to his touch. She wanted him to see what he'd been missing while making her wait days before seeing him. She enjoyed the phone calls, but phone sex wasn't sex, and she wanted, needed the touch of a man—this man. From her vantage point, he took good care of her, supplying her with gifts, cash, and even the deposit for her new apartment. She was accustomed to men taking from her, so being bought for the price of keeping her hair and nails done didn't strike her as cheap.

She combed the wrap from her hair and it bounced around her shoulders like she'd just left the shop. She sprayed on Halston, his favorite scent, and put on the lacy underwear and matching bra he'd bought her. 'Only wear these for me,' he'd whispered in her ear at the checkout while her girlish grin made the sales boy blush.

Tonight, he was coming to take her out. She'd been complaining about them meeting up at his friend's condo whenever he was away on business or at the Cabrini Green apartment, where her dad slept on the couch. She hated entertaining there, but he didn't seem to mind. He'd grown up in the projects and was used to the elements that would have given non-project-bred folks pause. He'd escaped the confines of that existence and started his own commercial maintenance business that included lucrative contracts with the city of Chicago. The Aldermen that helped him secure the contract was being taken care of monthly because that was just how business was done in Chicago. He revealed a lot about the windy city politics during their pillow talks, and she hung on every word.

She tried dating men her own age, but they possessed the misdirection and apathy she witnessed in her brothers and feared their fate would follow the same mass incarceration path or one to an early grave. She needed maturity, someone she could look up to, who would take care of her and be there for her when no one else would, like her father was. He gave all he had after her mother left; she knew he could have left, too. Left her and her brothers to become the Department of Child and Family Services' problem, wards of the state, but he sacrificed his own happiness to nurture Tina the best way he could and fill the void in her soul left by her mother's abandonment.

She stepped back and admired herself in the mirror. She'd selected her lowcut, crimson color dress. She bent over, positioning her cleavage into a perfect mound, and glanced over her shoulder at how the fabric cuddled her hips in a tight embrace.

He didn't take her out often. He was always tired from working so hard. Tina's image of the perfect family was filled by the television reruns of the white suburban households she watched growing up as a kid. The wife always there when the husband came home from work, with their aprons and clean kids and dinner on the dining room table. These were Tina's role models, the only examples she had of how a relationship was supposed to be. Those mothers stayed, took care of their families, and catered to their men. She cursed her mother for not being that way.

The doorbell rang, and she slid into three-inch heels and like Edith Bunker from her favorite re-run, she trotted to the door to answer it. He filled the room with his presence, reducing Tina's gregarious personality to a timid third-grader in awe of her favorite teacher. He threw his arms around her, lifting her short frame up to meet his lips, her feet dangling just above the floor, then he walked her over to the couch, bringing her side saddled across his lap. She didn't want to let go but gazed into his eyes, smiling from ear to ear.

His eyes rolled over her from head to toe. "Nice," he said, grinning at her while brushing the back of his hand over her well-placed cleavage. "Drink."

He smacked her butt as she rose on cue and entered the kitchen to make his drink just the way she'd watched the TV wives do it. She'd even taken to calling him honey. "Where we headed tonight, honey?" She asked, bringing him his drink and returning to make one for herself.

He had turned the television on, his attention divided between the news chatter of the successful Hands Across America campaign and the cocktail that Tina had fixed just right. He threw it back in one gulp, handing the empty glass to her as she returned with her own.

Tina placed her drink on a coaster and returned to the kitchen to fix him another, "You're keeping me in suspense about tonight, I see," she said, always finding excuses for him not listening to her when she talked. He was most engaged when he was doing the talking but fell aloof when she had something to say.

She returned with his drink to find him snoring lightly, his head slumped over to the side. Tina stood there, all dressed up, with his drink in her hand, before sitting beside him and quietly staring blankly into the TV as the news reporter gave updates on the Chernobyl explosion. She sipped her drink slowly, then slipped off her three-inch heels, and rested her head on his sleeping shoulders. Maybe they'd go out tomorrow night, she thought, as she finished her drink and then his too.

CHAPTER 5

I stood back and admired the various shades of white paint samples patched on the walls and moldings, trying to find one that evoked style but neutrality at the same time. It had been over three months since I signed my signature to the last document and watched as the escrow assistant tapped the mounds of mortgage documents on the table to even the edges. "I'll get your copies and your keys, and congratulations on your first home," she said as she left to make the copies.

It was my first home, but I had no intentions of living in it long. Leon, my loan officer, suggested the first-time homebuyer program as a way of lowering my monthly payments while I rehabbed it. "That's how the white boys do it," he'd said, feeling very comfortable and somewhat proud that he was helping a black woman do what white boys had been doing for years. He schooled me on the difference in the interest rate between investment property and first-time homeownership, convincing me to use the first-time homeowner status to make the investment even more profitable. There was no prepayment penalty and I'd have more money to put toward my next investment. If he was looking to gain my business for future transactions, he had sealed the deal.

I left the title office with my mountain of executed loan documents and keys in hand and drove straight to my new four-unit
apartment building. I would live in one of the units as I rehabbed
the others, then move temporarily into one of the rehabbed ones
until the last unit was completed. This would eliminate the rent I
was currently paying on my South Shore apartment. Thinking back
about how I'd kited a check to move into that apartment made me
laugh out loud as to how far I'd come. Those days, and meeting
Trace, who helped me through them, would shape my life forever.

I pulled up in front of the units and felt my heart skip a beat as
my eyes took in the tea-peed oak tree streaming with toilet paper
and spray paint sprawled across the brick façade. From the corner
of my eye, I saw the tenant that had to be forced to move out, jet
from the backyard with the spray can in his hand. I leaped from my
car and started chasing him.

"Hey, hey, stop. I see you. Stop." I yelled as he jetted across the
street, between two duplexes and down an alley. I clearly wasn't
thinking as I made pursuit, chasing behind him into the unknown,
before caging him in at a locked alley gate. He turned to face me,
the can of spray paint his only weapon; he started spraying the
paint my way. It was then that I noticed for the first time that he
was actually a she. She wore her hair pulled back and her jeans low
on her hips. Her baseball cap covered up what were beautiful brown
eyes encased in the longest natural eyelashes I'd ever seen.

"Get back," she said, spraying red paint into the air. "Help!" she
had the nerve to yell.

"Help!? You're kidding me, right? You destroy my property and
yell for help."

"You kicked me out. What am I supposed to do, huh? Where
I'm supposed to go?"

It wasn't until then that I noticed she was just a child. I'd only seen her in the distance when I sat in the car while my realtor explained that she would have to move out. She was tall but thin and from the distance, I didn't make out that it was a she or that she was all of sixteen years old. "Where are your parents?" I asked.

"Who knows?" she said, sputtering the last of the spray paint my way. "Ain't seen 'em in months. Used to find 'em strung out in a crack house, but ain't nobody down there seen them in a while. So, I got to do what I got to do, ya feel me."

It was like I was looking into my past. Feeling left alone in a world to fend for myself, except I had family to take me in. "You got family? Somewhere you can go?" I asked.

"Oh, now you all concerned? You kicked me out, remember?"

"I'm rehabbing the place; I can help you find somewhere to—"

"Whatever, lady," she said, tossing the can at me. "I can take care of myself."

I stepped aside to let her pass. The thought of her parents in the crack houses like the ones I'd seen when running with Trace made me shudder. I thought about Trace's son, Trevor, whose mother fell victim to the crack epidemic that was sweeping the country. Danny, learning of all of his siblings that Trace had conceived, was determined to be in their lives. He helped get Trevor placed in foster care with the same couple that had taken in his infant sibling, Josh. He was determined to adopt them both one day, but I had deep reservations about it. Particularly now that he was possibly contemplating running for office.

Something inside me moved. Sitting in church every Sunday as a child, and the strong faith that lifted me to my current situation poured out. "I can help you," I said.

"Naw. Thanks. Don't need it," she said, pushing past me.

"You want to end up like your parents," I said, stopping her in her tracks. I wasn't sorry that I said it. She was a teenager and a little tough love may go a long way. I wanted her to know she had options. "Or, you can accept the kindness of strangers. Unless you like sleeping under the L and being subjected to—"

"Ok, ok," she said. "But just for one night. I can take care of myself."

That was over three months ago and Charmaine had become like the little sister I never had. I'd learned a lot about the foster care system by helping Danny with Trevor. I called on the same caseworker that helped us get Trevor placed with his brother. She seemed genuinely concerned about the children she was assigned to and didn't disappoint when it came to Charmaine. She helped locate her parents, who both had been in Cook County jail awaiting trial for trying to rob a gas station for drug money. They had no way of calling in to check on Charmaine or let her know what happened to them, and I got the feeling they didn't even try. The caseworker worked her magic and got Charmaine in a girls' group home. She was sixteen and going into her junior year.

"These two," Charmaine said, referring to one of the white swatches of paint that I was agonizing over. "This one for the wall color, it's bright enough to lighten up the room and capture the morning glow from the east-facing windows."

Charmaine was over at the fourplex whenever the group home allowed free time before her curfew. She had an eye for decorating and her insight into how to make the best use of the space in each unit was a welcomed skill. My strength was negotiating the deals, and I was okay with that.

"White is white. Can't go wrong there," Danny said as Melvin, my contractor, marched into the room.

Danny had been spending most of the little free time he got off from work to help me reel in the contractor. A huge middle-aged black guy, who always reminded me that he'd been rehabbing buildings since before I was born, was of the impression that talking loud meant his opinion was the final say. I respected his expertise, but when it came to how I wanted the finished product to look visually, I had the final say. He threw his weight around, intending to intimidate me into agreeing to the shortcut he was trying to execute, primarily to keep the bulk of our agreed-upon fee in his pocket.

Melvin walked up to me, planting his burly frame in my personal space. "I'm thinking we can paint the guest bathroom walls but leave the woodwork as is. See, no need in spending time on that, they look fine," he said.

"Fresh painted walls will make the moldings look worn if not painted. So, I think we should definitely—"

"Hey man, tell her ain't no use in painting them moldings in there, for crying out loud," he said, looking at Danny as if I, the person writing his checks, wasn't standing there.

I held my ground. "We were just talking about how the wall color made the moldings pop, so we want to make—"

Melvin sucked his teeth, "Come here, man. Let me show you what I'm talking about." He turned his back on me and headed back up the stairs.

Danny squeezed my hand as he made his way behind him, "Let me talk to him."

Charmaine rolled her eyes, "Men be tripping, always think they know shit and they be wrong as hell. Can't tell 'em nothing. They make me sick."

"Yeah, can't live with them, can't live without them, as the saying goes," I said.

"I can live without 'em," she said as Danny made his way back downstairs.

He threw his hands up, "He gets it now. Done deal, Moldings painted."

"Thanks, Danny. You need to remind him that I write the checks," I said.

"Sure, baby. You're the boss," he responded. His tone hit me as condescending as Melvin's.

Charmaine gave me the side-eye; his tone wasn't lost on her either. "I'm outta of here. Registering for classes today," she said, slinging her bag over her shoulder and heading out the door. "I'll catch y'all later."

Danny watched as she closed the door behind her and then pointed toward the patches of paint on the wall. "You good with the selection she made?"

I nodded. "Why?"

"Nothing, just that. Well, you really don't know anything about her, and her parents are all locked up, from what I can tell, will be for a while, too.

"And?" I said, clocking his judgmental tone.

"Just looking out for you. That's all," he said, throwing his hands up.

"I appreciate that. She's just a teenage girl, that—"

"Girl?" Danny laughed. "You sure about that?"

"Don't be mean," I said, remembering the mean girls who teased me in middle school for just being me.

"You don't know her from Adam, and I—"

"Whoa, wait a minute. You didn't know Trevor, Candice, Little Ray—"

"That's different—"

"Josh or Rhonda," I said, my fingers counting out Trace's kids, Danny's newfound siblings.

"They're family, no compar—"

"That you knew nothing about. How's that different than my helping Charmaine? Trevor's parents were crackheads, and that—"

"Look, forget it. Just don't come crying to me when—"

"Crying to you? When have I—"

"How about today! Can't handle your own damn contractors. I told you this rehab stuff was too much right now on top of wedding planning. Supposed to be meeting my Mom for a dress fitting today, right?" he said, checking his watch. "But naw, you focused on some damn paint colors."

I just looked at him. These seemingly unprovoked outrages were beginning to paint his personality.

"You should've put the money in an IRA like I suggested. Less headache and less—"

"—return on my investment. And excuse me, I didn't know you felt that asking for your help was crying on your shoulders. Thanks for letting me know," I said.

"Now you're putting words in my mouth. I'm out." He stormed out the door.

"Words in your... Those were your words?" I said, marching behind him. "Danny, wait, we can't just leave it like this. What is wrong with you?"

"I'm just trying to help you, Sinclair. But your head is so damn hard, got this strange dike girl hanging around here, and—"

"Don't call her that—"

"—dealing with these jackleg contractors. You determined you gonna do it your way. So, do it," he said as he got into his car. "Don't let Mom tell me you left her waiting for that fitting."

"Danny, wait. Really! What is your problem?"

But I was talking to myself. He revved his engine and peeled off down the street, leaving me standing on the sidewalk trying to figure out what the hell just happened. In the past, he'd blamed this unprovoked behavior on the huge class load he was taking, then after graduation, on the cases that were piling on. Now, with the wedding planning and his Mom making changes that he and I had agreed on before, not to mention her pressuring him to run for office, was certainly not helping matters.

I had just enough time to make it back to the South Shore apartment to change before meeting Carla, Jasmine and Tina for my fitting.

The wedding dress boutique was decorated like a princess drawing room. The chandeliers hung over a white shag rug in a room with pink lounge chairs for the bridal guest. The attendant had laid out several dresses for me based on our previous phone call. When I arrived, Carla had also made her own selections that she had the attendant present to me and insisted I try on first.

"Looks like you're going to a seventeenth-century Debutant Ball," Tina said without remorse.

"It's not that bad," Jasmine said, holding in a laugh.

I turned on the platform looking at the dress that Carla had selected. It was a princess dress with layers of tulle around the bottom and a fitted bodice of lace and silk, with more tulle over the bust and shoulders finished off with silk ruffles on a high neck.

Carla stood with her hands clasped at her chin, beaming with joy, "I think it's beautiful. Danny will love it."

The sales clerk must have had experience with future mothers-in-law and saved me from the awkward moment.

"We have so many wonderful selections to choose from," the sales clerk said, helping me off the podium.

I rushed to the dressing room to remove the hideous garment that I wouldn't be caught dead in at a Halloween ball, less alone at my wedding. I would have to find a way, subtle or not, of letting

Carla know that the dress was my decision and mine alone. Her support over the last few months had been a bittersweet mix of welcome contributions to grossly overstepping her bounds, and today was one of those days.

I slipped into a fitted gown, intricate lace over a satin lining, the bodice was adorned with hand-sewn pearls, accented with satin trim over an off the shoulders bust line. The train trailed six feet and was embellished with matching pearls. The sales girl fastened the satin buttons that ran down the back of the dress from shoulder to hips. I admired myself in the mirror before walking out to the showroom.

Jasmine's eyes watered when I walked onto the podium. "Sinclair. That's so beautiful."

"That's what I'm talking about," Tina said. "Show off them curves, girl."

I admired myself in the three-way mirror, doing half-turns from side-to-side when I caught Carla's reflection. She clocked me from my head to toe, her poker expression concealing her feelings. She wasn't beaming like she was when I was in the other dress, and she didn't say anything about how much Danny would love it.

"I think this is it," I refused to let her sour face be the memory I have of this moment. "I'll take it," I said.

We'd planned lunch together before taking Carla to the airport for her flight back to D.C., but she excused herself, claiming she had business in Chicago to attend to before catching her flight. We air-kissed as we parted ways in the Magnificent Mile. She'd remained pretty quiet after the fitting and I hoped she'd get over it. She had proven to be a valuable source in the wedding planning, but that was not synonymous with controlling everything. I was sure she understood that.

Over lunch, the girls didn't waste any time offering their unsolicited opinions as we sipped mimosas.

"Mommy Dearest is pissed off now," Jasmine said, extending her hand toward Tina,

"For real, Girl!" Tina slapped Sinclair's extended hand. "Hide the hangers."

I felt it was easier to join them than to beat them. "Carla loves to be in control, that's for sure."

"No kidding, Sherlock," Jasmine said, raising a glass of orange juice to her lips, then looking at it with disdain. "Look, I'm gonna need something stronger than this orange juice." She waved the waitress over. "I'll take a Screwdriver. Y'all good," she asked Tina and me.

"I'm good. No Vodka for breakfast for me," Tina said.

Jasmine gave Tina the side-eye. "We're well into lunch," she said.

We were enjoying lunch at our favorite spot in the Magnificent Mile. Hooking up on the weekends was our signature girlfriend thing to do and we spared no expense. Jasmine was preparing for graduation and seriously thinking about starting her own Management Consulting firm.

"How's business, boss lady?" I asked as she gulped down her cocktail and waved to the waiter for another.

"Busy. Still holding down my sales job until graduation and I can get the business off the ground. Looking for an assistant to help with the workload. If y'all know anyone, send them my way."

"Dang, an assistant. Scared of you," Tina said.

"There's just so much going on. Ain't no shame in my game. I can't keep up with it on my own. Need somebody that can take care of the details. Make sure things don't fall through the cracks."

"What about Charmaine," I said. "She's sharp as a tack. And talented in so many areas."

I didn't miss the look that Tina and Jasmine shared between them.

"What?" I asked.

"Well…" Tina said, cocking her head as if I could read some undefined sign language.

"What? Since when you at a loss for words," I said.

"You think she might be funny?" Jasmine blurted out as the waiter set her drink down. He stiffened at the comment.

I looked at Jasmine sideways, waiting on the waiter to leave, then whispered, "I think they call it gay now, and I don't know. I didn't ask her."

"Hell, you don't have to ask. It's obvious." Tina said.

"So, what if she is?"

"Forget I said anything, Sinclair. You seem to be a magnet for that type, anyway," Tina said, excusing her comment with the wave of a hand.

My ears heard the words, but my brain didn't put them together right away. It was like I had entered into the middle of a conversation being had by strangers. Trying to understand the context of something being said that I lacked pertinent details about.

"Magnet. For. That. Type," I repeated slowly, searching for how those four words grouped together had anything to do with me.

Tina rolled her eyes, "Yeah, girl. Tony?"

I shook my head, still clueless about the context. "What about Tony?" His name flooding back memories of how our time spent together went from heaven to hell overnight.

Tina looked at Jasmine, "You didn't tell her?"

Jasmine shrugged, "She's been through a lot, and now with planning the wedding. It didn't seem like—"

"Tell me what?"

"You said you were going to tell her. She needs—"

"Stop talking about me like I'm not sitting here. What the hell is going on? What about Tony?" I said.

They stared at each other as Jasmine took a swig of her drink and Tina nibbled on an appetizer.

"Fucking answer me," I yelled. People sitting near us stopped and looked our way.

Jasmine laid her hand on mine and looked deep into my eyes. It was that look she gave me whenever she had to tell me that Kyle was back in prison or when Aunt Mattie had died. She bit her lip and squeezed my hand. "Tony has AIDS, sweetie. He and one of Tina's brothers were locked up together. He's very sick."

Everything in the restaurant started to spin around like I was on a carnival ride. The waiter delivered the food to the table, but my appetite had been sucked out of me by the lump in my throat. This deadly disease had killed Hollywood sex symbol Rock Hudson just a year before, and the thought of me facing that same death sentence made sweat pour down my brow and cut off my capacity to breathe. In a haze, I removed myself from my seat, placing one foot in front of the other toward the bathroom, where the lump exploded from my chest into a cry of agony as Jasmine and Tina entered just in time to catch me as I collapsed into their arms.

CHAPTER 6

The simmering smell of garlic, onions and peppers drifted from the kitchen, shifting Jasmine's focus from her term paper to Doc's self-proclaimed award-winning chili. The scent trigging memories from her childhood of Grandmama Pearl's down-home cooking.

"Always start with the trinity," Grandmama Pearl would say, "You can't end wrong if you start out like that."

Didn't matter if you were cooking chili, spaghetti, black-eyed peas or collard greens, the trinity was a signature base from her childhood cooking lessons that made Jasmine halfway believe Doc's tall tales about his award-winning chili recipe. He'd come over to cook for her while she worked on her term paper. Managing to work his way, without any objection from her, into her apartment, her sacred space not shared with many, especially random men.

She'd made her apartment her sanctuary. It represented the peace that juxtaposed her traumatic childhood that she fought to overcome as an adult by surrounding herself with beautiful things. She didn't look at life as being unable to afford something like most folks did. For Jasmine, it was all about enjoying the best life had to offer and feeling one hundred percent like she deserved whatever she wanted and the universe would see that she would have it.

Her apartment was filled with artwork from the hottest new artist and designer furniture from the finest galleries. Bright, bold colors cast a calm presence over her environment and eased the chatter of past hurt and pain. Her undergraduate degree, and multiple sales awards from work, accented the entryway of her apartment. She wanted all who entered to know that she was to be taken seriously, and if they felt intimidated by that, then they were in the wrong place dealing with the wrong black woman.

Doc had entered her apartment for the first time with a bag of groceries and her favorite wine. He wrapped her in his arms and pressed his lips to hers in a passionate kiss. Looking around the room, he took in her space. The scented candles and fresh flowers collided in a bouquet of fragrance, and an eye candy of tasteful décor and picturesque views of Lake Michigan lay stretched out through her twenty-story windows.

"Gonna make you some of my award-winning chili," he said, holding up the grocery bag.

Jasmine looped her arms through his, guiding him into the kitchen, "What award would that be?" she asked, pulling a corkscrew from the drawer.

"Turner Family reunion, undefeated champ, three years running," he said, popping the cork from the bottle of red wine.

Doc Turner was a big man with a baby face that defied his demanding voice. It was that baritone voice that hooked Jasmine the second he said hello at the skating rink. At first, she didn't let on, ignoring him, chalking him up for a common south side low rent negro. But his sexy voice, charming disposition, and eyes that sparkled brighter than the stars in a country sky disarmed her, letting him penetrate her usually unbreakable barrier.

The smell coaxed her from her studies and she made her way into the kitchen. She stood at the doorway watching Doc, who had found one of Grandmama Pearl's aprons in a drawer and draped it around his waist. He was humming and stirring a pot. Jasmine giggled at the sight of him in her grandmama's apron.

He turned and smiled at her. "You won't be laughing once you taste this magical chili," he said as he watched Jasmine pour herself another glass of wine. She tipped the bottle his way. "I'm good for now," he said. I like to enjoy my wine when I'm eating my chili. Maybe I should have bought two bottles, though."

Jasmine opened up a cabinet revealing a well-stocked wine cooler and pulled out another bottle of red. "There's no shortage here, counselor," she said.

She had learned a lot about Doc in the few months since meeting him. The most surprising was that Doc was his actual name. His father named him with aspirations of him becoming a doctor. He grew up in a predominately black neighborhood in North St. Louis and was introduced to the juvenile justice system when he was fifteen. His father had drilled in him that trouble was easy to get into and hard to get out of, but Doc didn't think that far ahead when he joined a group of boys on a joy ride in a stolen car. He was charged with grand theft auto and was facing time in juvenile detention. His father, a Jamaican immigrant, was the head of maintenance in a downtown law firm, and that connection proved to be the saving grace that Doc needed. A lawyer in the firm, who thought highly of Beaumont Turner, Doc's father, represented Doc for free and was able to get him off on probation. The other boys, whose families lacked the connections and the means to pay for quality representation, were sent away to juvenile detention and caught up in the school-to-prison pipeline system that rounded up black inner-city youths like cattle.

Being locked up for the two nights that it took his family to raise the bail money was enough to scare Doc straight. That was the first and last time he saw the inside of a jail cell. He didn't live up to his father's expectations of becoming a medical doctor, but he did attend college and went on to get his Masters in Social Work, where he now fought for young black men as a high school counselor. Sharing his father's wise words with them, trouble is easy to get into and hard to get out of.

Jasmine was fascinated by Doc and how easily he meshed his tough North St. Louis swagger with the caring high school counselor role. A black man with an MSW was sexy as hell to her. She set the table for two, complete with candles and soft music, as Doc swung open her kitchen cabinets until he found a serving dish for the chili. She felt unsarcastically at ease watching him make himself at home in her space, letting herself relax in his presence and this simple act of preparing a meal with him.

"Let me get that," Doc said, reaching above Jasmine's head to get the bowls out of the cabinet. "As a matter of fact," he said, pulling out a chair for her to sit at the table, "I'm serving you tonight."

Jasmine sat down on cue as Doc opened the second bottle of wine. "Let's let that breath a minute," he said, as he placed the serving bowl of chili on the table and scoped a healthy serving into the bowls, "You are in for a treat, baby girl."

Jasmine somehow knew that, in more ways than one, he was right about one thing, the chili was award-winning, It had a spice that she couldn't quite put her finger on, and Doc wasn't giving up his secret.

"It's in the sauce," he said, winking at her. "If I tell ya, I got kill ya."

After dinner, they sat on the couch, the friendly back and forth of agreements and disagreement flowed smoothly between them.

Jasmine couldn't remember the last time she engaged in such meaningful conversation with a man. She wasn't sure if it was because she seldom opened herself up. For the longest time, she viewed men as sex objects, mainly to keep from putting herself out there and getting hurt. But Doc had certainly put a crack in her shield, and she was enjoying every minute of it. She wasn't sure when, but she had stopped listening to him speak and was just watching his lips move. A dimple formed beneath his nose, creating a heart-shaped mound that sat perfectly above his top lip, screaming to be kissed. Jasmine leaned in and Doc stopped talking in mid-sentence, his face meeting hers as they kissed for the first time. They'd gone out on several dates, but Doc had been the perfect gentleman. Jasmine wanted him to take her and have his way with her. They kissed hard, and Jasmine moved closer, pressing her breast against him. Doc pulled her into him and they both moaned as the kiss took them deeper and deeper into the moment. Jasmine straddled him and as soon as the passion inside her was about to explode, Doc lifted her with his strong arms and backed away.

Jasmine opened her eyes, "What's wrong?"

"You have to finish that paper," he said, adjusting his manhood in his pants."

"Let me worry about that," Jasmine said, reaching for him.

Doc stood up, taking her hand and lifting her to meet him. "I want you, I do. But I'm looking for more than the joy of your body. I'm looking for the joy of knowing all of you, mind, body and soul. We'll get there, but you can't rush fine wine, baby."

He walked her to the door, kissed her lips and whispered, " I can't wait to have you."

He opened the door and left, leaving Jasmine all hot and bothered. She went into her bedroom, retrieved her toy from the bedside table, and pleasured herself, screaming out Doc's name as she climaxed and released the pint-up energy that her grueling school studies and work impinged on her. She smiled to herself, feeling swept away by the romance of being courted by someone who wanted to know her innermost feelings—mind, body and soul.

She went back into the kitchen and poured herself another glass of wine, cracked open her books, and started studying.

CHAPTER 7

I sat in my car staring out the window at a woman and a small child racing across the street to get out of the rain. The smell of rain always reminded me of being home in Gary. Jasmine, Kyle and me playing games on the front porch, waiting for the rain to stop and the sun to peep out from behind the clouds so we could run back to the playground to finish our kickball game or whatever we were playing before the rain interrupted our fun. Sometimes, the other kids in the neighborhood would join us on the porch to play marbles or pick up sticks, and Grandmama Pearl would make Kool-Aid and peanut butter and jelly sandwiches for everyone. She loved the rain too, said it reminded her of being back on the farm down south where she grew up. But, If it started lightning, she'd make us all come inside and sit still. We couldn't even talk to each other. Talking would get us struck by the lighting, she warned us, and as kids, we believed everything Grandmama Pearl said. So, we sat still—no TV, no radio, no talking until the lighting stopped because none of us wanted to be set on fire by lightning.

I often think of Grandmama Pearl and her wise tales and superstitions. She believed wholeheartedly in what she believed in, and it was not open for discussion. She didn't have much of an education but was smart as a whip and had a discernment that I figured came only with grey hair and bunions. She could peg a person's character in the time that it took them to tip their hat, and with time it was proven that she was almost always right. I wondered what she would have said about Danny. I missed the lesson born out of her wisdom and wished she was here to give me her unsolicited opinion.

I'd been parked in front of Danny's place for close to an hour, debating if I should knock on his door or let him continue to pout. It had been over a week since Carla had told him her side of the story about my dress fitting. On top of that, his feathers were still ruffled about my rehabbing the fourplex.

The rain subsided and I opened the car door, stuck my umbrella out and popped it open. I'd just gotten my hair done. I'd cut it short after leaving Kahn. In search of a new look and finding a new me. I let go of my thick curls and opted for tapered sides and back with a long bang swept to the side. I don't think Danny ever forgave me for cutting my hair. He never said he didn't like it. Just kept looking at my hair when he saw me, making no comment about it one way or the other, but his look and silence said it all. Like now, his silence was his way of telling me he was not happy about the choices I made regarding the fourplex and apparently my own damn wedding dress. I wasn't sure how long his silent treatment was supposed to last, but I was putting an end to it today. We had appointments with the venue and caterers coming up. I made it clear that his mother couldn't serve as a substitute for all of the wedding planning that he and I had agreed we'd do together.

I punched in the entry code on the door and let myself into the lobby of his apartment building. It was a three-story walk up and I made my way to the third floor. Standing before Danny's door, I wondered if I should have come. If I should have just been still and waited for this storm to pass like Grandmama Pearl made us do in the rain, but this silence was killing me, so I opted for the lightning.

The middle ground, the not knowing what the silent treatment meant in the end was more torturous than the lightning itself. The scenarios I'd conjured up in my head invaded my thoughts every waking minute. The more I tried to put it out of my mind, the more it haunted me. I was tired of feeling that way and needed him to use his damn words so that we could move on.

I raised my hand to knock, but the door swung open instead. Danny stood there in sweats and a t-shirt. His scowl was like a dagger to my heart and cast a feeling of defeat over me.

"Was wondering how long you were going to sit in that car," he said, walking into the living room.

I stood there, watching him, knowing in my bones what Grandmama Pearl would say about any man that behaved that way, but I was too close to the forest to see the trees. "If you saw me, why didn't you invite me up?" I said, maintaining my position in the doorway.

"You coming in or what?"

I debated if I should come in or not, given his stormy attitude. I was a bit terrified by what I saw. "What's up, Danny? What's wrong with you, for real?"

"Ain't nothing up. Been busy," he said, walking over to the couch and sitting down. "Me and Mom been talking to folks about the Alderman run, you know?"

My legs finally moved and I made my way inside but stood by the door, uncomfortable with how uncomfortable I felt before the man I was about to marry.

"Shut the door," he said, taking a swig from his beer.

I shut the door as he demanded and walked toward the couch. I was dumbfounded. I wanted to scream at him but didn't want to make matters any worse than they obviously already were. "So, you are running for office? Alderman?" I managed to say. "Carla mentioned that. We hadn't talked—"

"Ms. Boone."

"Excuse me?"

"I think you should call my Mom, Ms. Boone."

He'd gone from the sublime to the ridiculous, but I'd been hypnotized by his charm and couldn't call him out on his nonsense. "Is that what she wants?"

He shrugged, "Just respectable, that's all. Is that a problem?"

"Being respectable isn't a problem at all. Being demeaned is, and—"

Danny threw up his hands, "Oh, here we go."

"Yes, here we go. I've been calling her Carla. She herself told me I could. So, I don't know what you tripping about, but I think it's time you lose this juvenile behavior and deal with me like a grown-ass man. What's your problem, Danny?"

"Why you keep asking me that?

I took a deep breath. I wasn't going to let him take me there. Aunt Matte always told us it took two to argue. I quickly weighed my options; what was the real issue here? I needed to deal with that. "When were you going to tell me that you plan to run for Alderman? Don't you think that's something that I should know?"

He shrugged, swigged his beer and shifted in his seat. I let the silence lay between us for several uncomfortable seconds. "Danny?"

I was thrust back to Uncle Ervin and Aunt Mattie, watching how he would completely ignore her when he didn't want to deal with what she was saying. I would have to hold my tongue to keep from shouting at him, "Don't you hear her talking to you?" Aunt

Mattie would stand there with her hands on her hips, shifting back and forth from one foot to the other, her hands crossed, then back to her hips, calling his name, "Ervin, Ervin! I know you hear me talking to you." The flashback put a knot in my stomach and I knew it was time for me to leave. I had nothing more to say and was damned if I was going to be Aunt Mattie.

Without saying a word, I got up and walked toward the door.

"Where you going?" Danny said.

"Anywhere but here," I said, reaching for the doorknob.

Danny sprinted across the room, placing himself between me and the door.

"You holding me against my will, now? Get out of the way, Danny. I'm tired of your—"

He stood there, not able to even look me in the face. He shifted from one foot to the other like a middle-school boy in trouble with the principal. "I wasn't planning to run for Alderman. Mom, when she was here for the Taste of Soul, I guess you can say she got a taste of Chicago politics. Anyway, she suggested it would be a good idea to run for Alderman. You know, a good move for my career and a way to accelerate my run for Chicago District Attorney," he said, looking down at his feet.

At least now I had his attention and took advantage of my offensive position. "A decision like that impacts me, too," I said softly, trying to match the vulnerable disposition that had replaced the nasty attitude he'd greeted me with.

Like Dr. Jackal and Mr. Hide, Danny glared at me. "So, you don't want to support me! I support your property flipping and picking up stray teenage, whatever the hell—"

"Don't try to beat me getting mad! Why didn't you tell me!?" I demanded.

He ran his hands through his thick hair, "It happened so fast.

Mom filed the paperwork, and the next thing I know, I was meeting people and talking about campaign strategy, and I just got all wrapped up in the excitement of it all."

I became suddenly aware that Carla was a problem I would need to manage. Her meddling in our lives was a liability that could take Danny and me out if not dealt with. I wasn't losing the man I loved over some controlling mother. One way to do that was to control him myself. "Do you want to run?" I asked, adjusting my tone. The last thing I wanted to do was to sound like Carla.

"He looked at me with schoolboy eyes and shrugged. "I'm so busy and confused, Sinclair. I just want to work my way through the system and become a kick-ass prosecutor. I know the Alderman route is one way, but… I just don't want to disappoint my mom; she's done so much for me."

I wrapped my hands around him, and he rested his head on my shoulder.

"I just don't want to disappoint her," he repeated. "I love you so much, and I'm sorry that I've been acting an ass. I knew I should have spoken with you about it, but—"

"Look, I get it. Your mother wants the best for you, and your wanting to give it to her is what any dedicated son would want. But we're getting married. It's me and you, babe. You want that District Attorney seat?

He nodded into my shoulder.

"Then we get you in it together, but not through some back alley, thankless, city Alderman job. We're going straight to the top." He looked into my eyes and I stared into his soul, "But we do it, together. Do you trust me?"

He nodded, "But, how do I tell her. I don't want—"

"We'll tell her together. But you have to promise me, never let anyone, not even your mama, come between us again."

Danny wrapped me in is arms. "When you walked toward that door, man, the thought of you walking out of my life—"

"Naw, you're not getting rid of me that easy."

We stood there holding each other. The relief that swept over me at odds with the discomfort about Carla and the hold she had on her son. I'd managed to break the spell she cast upon me when we first met at the Taste of Chicago, but Danny had lived with her manipulation his entire life. I knew breaking that bond would be an uphill battle, but I was also confident that loosening her grip was within reach with a little strategic maneuvering. Starting with Danny and I making up for lost time and doing the one thing for him that Carla could never do.

Danny and I walked into the tasting room of the cake bakery, holding hands and finishing each other's sentences as we chatted about the reception venue we'd just visited. The ballroom for our wedding reception was beautiful, with wall-to-ceiling glass doors encased in mahogany leading out into a veranda overlooking Lake Michigan. Crystal droplets hung from the chandeliers over hand-sewn Moroccan carpets. The dance floor, which we agreed was the biggest draw, faced the stage where the band and DJ would play our favorite songs. We were looking forward to tasting the delicious cakes and ending this beautiful day of planning our wedding together. We'd renewed our relationship after confessing that he didn't want to run for Alderman and had become closer than ever. Planning our future together had become his number one priority.

Carla offered no resistance to our venue decision. "It's a lovely place and, when decorated, will make for some memorable photos," she said as we drove to the bakery. She'd come into town with the plan to introduce Danny to some high roller political fundraisers, but Danny and I agreed that we'd tell her over dinner that he would not be running for Alderman,

I often thought of Trace and what he would think about his son, the attorney. About the man Carla raised and controlled with the gesture of her manicured finger. I'd seen how Trace dealt with his sons, Little Ray and Trevor, and he wouldn't have accepted the coddling and smothering way that Carla had raised Danny. I realized that she'd done the best she could without Trace or any other man having her back. The way single women raised their daughters and loved their sons was like night and day and contributed to a pool of what Grandmama Pearl called, man babies.

Danny, Carla and I tasted the cakes and sipped the complimentary bottle of champagne the baker had provided. I smiled at Carla, who was on her best behavior. I no longer trusted her any further than I could throw her, so my smile harbored as much callousness as hers, just a lot more undercover. She had no idea that Danny and I were about to shut her and her Alderman fiasco down. Secretly, I wanted her to be blind-sided so that she would understand in no uncertain terms, who was running this show.

We finished our tasting and walked the short two blocks to the restaurant, where we had reservations for dinner. As usual, Carla walked between us, our arms linked through hers. When first meeting her, when she first pulled this maneuver, I felt accepted, but now I felt manipulated, knowing that it was a part of her controlling arsenal. Her way of keeping her foot on Danny's neck and letting any woman that got close to him know that she would always be in the middle of their business.

I stopped, faking tying the strings on my boot, and when I stood back up, I maneuvered my way next to Danny's side, positioning myself in the middle. I smiled slyly, proud of myself when she rolled her eyes my way. I was glad because now I had her attention.

I made sure we were seated at the restaurant so that I could look dead into Danny's eyes. I cocked my head toward Carla. A sign for him to take the lead of the discussion. He narrowed his eyes and lifted his palms my way. I narrowed mine back—"Now!" they were saying, I've waited long enough.

Carla, as usual, took the lead. "Daniel, I've made appointments for us to have lunch tomorrow with Harold Washington's campaign manager. He's the best in the city and will almost guarantee—"

I was about to burst, "Carla!" I said louder than I intended to. She cranked her head my way and met my eyes head-on. We stared each other down for a second before I said, "Danny has something to tell you.'

Carla looked at Danny, her smile wrapped in manipulation, "What is it, son?"

Danny sat there, his eyes shifting between Carla and me, his ambivalence seeping through his pores. For a moment, I felt bad for him. Sorry that his mother had her claws in him so much that he would deny his own happiness. He was the total opposite of his father. Trace was all about his own happiness, the pleasures in life that brought him joy. The flip side of that was he cared less about the people he hurt in the process, from his baby's mamas to his children, his happiness was more important than others. Danny, on the other hand, cared deeply about others and their feelings; I could see the pain in his eyes as he sat there, contemplating the hurt he would bring to either one of us if his response didn't meet our expectations.

"I don't think I want to run for Alderman," he said, looking down at his drink. He picked it up, gulped it down and sat there staring at the empty glass.

"Think?" Carla said. She cut her eyes toward me, "or been persuaded?"

"The only thing I was persuaded to do was to get wrapped in a goal that's not mine, I—"

"Exactly what are your goals, then?"

"Mom, we've been over this. Please calm down—"

Carla slammed her napkin onto the table, "Don't tell me to calm down, son." She grabbed her purse and rose to her feet. "I hope you don't regret this," she said, glaring at me, "And I don't just mean the Alderman run." She pivoted on her pumps and marched out of the restaurant,

I looked over at Danny, who was still staring into his cocktail glass. I wanted to feel triumphant, like I had finally slain the dragon, but I felt more like I had taken a baby bird from its nest before its time.

Chapter 8

Tony ran his hands over his bald head. He'd shaved his hair off when spending time in the state prison before being moved to the Federal Penitentiary in Greenville, Illinois. He was indoctrinated quickly into the harsh reality of the consequences of his crimes while at state. He thought a bald head would make him look tough enough to avoid the harassment inflicted upon his fellow inmates but learned quickly that his stigma preceded him—his frail body and sores on his face were an all too familiar sign of the deadly disease that had become the death sentence for inmates, forced or unforced, into homosexual prison encounters. He was tarnished goods and nobody would touch him, not even sit next to him in the mess hall. He'd found his tribe among the other infected inmates who were cast out to serve their sentences in a prison within a prison.

A buzzer sounded, signaling his cue to stand by his cell door. When it slid open, he and the other men stepped out into the corridor, their hardened faces staring straight ahead. At the sound of a guard's command, they pivoted in unison and marched down the corridor, stopping on yet another command, every minute of their lives dictated by buzzers and commands stripping them of any taste of freedom.

The men filed into the waiting room and searched for their loved ones. Tony stood at the door, a bit confused. He hadn't had a visitor since being transferred to Greenville. His father, a pastor of fifty years in the church Tony grew up in as a preacher's kid, had come and prayed for his soul while he was still in lock up. The thought of his son having broken the law was a sin he felt forgivable, but for the sin of what his father called sexual blasphemy, he could never forgive. He'd laid his hands-on Tony and prayed for his healing. That was the last time Tony would ever see him. He gained solace that his mother was not alive to witness the shame he had brought on the family. He was an only child and had resigned himself to dying in prison alone.

Tony spotted her on a bench near the window. He gasped for breath and fought back the tears that stung his eyes. He was frozen in his prison-issued slip-on sneakers until the inmate behind him shoved him to move forward. He made his way across the room and sat down across from her, taking in her beauty, and how her new haircut made her cheekbones pop. He sniffed in the cologne she was wearing and felt a little turned on by the red nail polish she wore. "Sinclair, what are you doing here?" he finally said.

"Not the greeting I was expecting," she said, studying his face.

Tony covered his sores with his hand. "Not the visit I was expecting." He focused on his chewed-up nails. A childhood habit he'd once broken had come back after being locked up. He'd nibbled his nails to inches below his fingertips making the surrounding skin sore and red from the constant gnawing. He started picking at it, avoiding eye contact.

"You can't even look at me?" Sinclair said, a slow brewing storm under her calm demeanor.

Tony transfixed his eyes on his bleeding index finger. This was the woman he thought would be his wife. He'd fallen in love with her and had already made up in his mind that he would ask her to marry him. When Carter seduced him and unleashed a part of him he thought years of praying had freed him of, he couldn't overcome the shame and guilt. Learning about his diagnoses left him helpless and defeated. The shame he felt and the fear that he might have given Sinclair HIV clouded his discernment. When he acted on the insider trading tip that Carter had given him, he hoped the benefits that Sinclair would reap would be a path toward her forgiveness.

"Look at me, Tony!" Sinclair screamed. Alerting a guard who cautioned her to keep it down. "Look at me!" she whispered, not holding back the tears that ran down her cheeks. "That's the least you can do."

Tony complied, slowly lifting his face to meet hers. He used the back of his nibbled fingers to wipe away his tears before other inmates could see his weakness. He opened his mouth to speak, he wanted to say he was sorry, but the words seemed minute compared to the harm he had caused. He wanted to tell her he loved her, but it seemed ironic considering the acts that brought them both to this place. He'd had laid in his bunk many a night worrying that he had given Sinclair AIDS. He'd started more than a dozen letters to her, each tossed in the trash. He couldn't bring himself to reach out to her. He'd seen her in the courtroom during his sentencing, and the look on her face was forever burned into his mind. The look of disappointment and disgust. The way his father looked at him. The thought of Sinclair feeling the same way about him that his father did was an unbearable reality that he didn't have the strength to face.

Sinclair gazed into his eyes and found a hint of the man she once knew buried deep behind the shame he carried, but his soul was fading. Her anger melted into sorrow, then pity for him. It was hard not to compare everyone she knew to Trace. Though he wasn't perfect, he was comfortable in his skin and right with his soul. A trait she now knew was more important to her than college degrees and fancy titles. She needed confidence in her life, boldness and the freedom to be, whatever the hell it was, no matter who didn't like it.

She reached for Tony's hand before the guard yelled again, this time to demand no touching. She placed her hand on her heart as a sign of understanding Tony's pain.

"Are you... Do you have—" Tony said.

"No. I tested negative. I just came to say..." Sinclair thought it best to change her course. "I came to see how you're doing. How you holding up?" She felt no comfort in kicking this man that was already down.

"I don't have long left. I've been so worried about you—"

"Don't spend another second doing that—worrying about me. I forgive you, Tony. You're free. Enjoy whatever time you have left knowing that whatever cage they put you in, you're free."

The buzzer sounded and visitors began to collect themselves. Sinclair smiled at Tony and rose to her feet. "You keep your head up. I'm praying for you."

Tony lifted his head and smiled, and for the first time in a long time, he felt shameless and free.

The guards led the visitors out as the inmates were herded against the wall. Sinclair looked over her shoulder as Tony waved his goodbye. She found comfort in the smile he now had on his face, even if it would be short-lived. She'd come with the intent of giving Tony a piece of her mind. To make herself feel better about him putting her through so much pain. But God's plan prevailed, and instead, she was able to make him feel better, if only for a short while.

CHAPTER 9

I drove in silence back to Chicago. Partly because I needed to hear myself think, but mainly because the radio in my car was on the blink. I'd sunk all of my money into my fourplex, putting off the purchase of a new car. The 1973 Monte Carlo I drove had served me well, and I was hoping to squeeze a few more miles out of it before having to buy a new car. I had cut out a picture of a Mercedes Benz from a magazine and taped it to my bathroom wall as a reminder of where I was headed. I was glad to put Tony behind me and was looking forward to a bright future.

Work on the fourplex was moving slower than I wanted, thanks to Melvin, the contractor from hell; I was behind schedule for completing the rehab. Charmaine's help with kitchen and bathroom décor was an added bonus; she was blossoming into a straight-A student and model resident at the halfway house. She'd been able to connect with her parents in county jail as they awaited trial. With Reagan in the White House and his war on drugs rhetoric, her addicted parents didn't stand a chance of acquittal, but Charmaine hoped for a light sentence, even though she had shared with me that she felt they deserved whatever they got. "They don't like me anyway," she said.

"That's ridiculous," I told her. "Parents love their children, no matter how hard things get."

"Not mine," Charmaine said, holding up the tile sample she was considering.

"Your parents have a lot going on. You're not in your right mind when on that crack, trust me," I said.

"They ain't always been on crack. Before they got hooked, my dad was always calling me a bull dyke, claiming he was just teasing. Said I looked butch, and he'd be glad when I grew out of it. I was only eleven, twelve years old, and was teased enough in school, didn't need him doing it at home. Old Girl thought it was funny. When they started getting high, their favorite pass time, next to hitting that pipe, was picking on me. Old man said he was going to beat that funny out of me, and Moms didn't do nothing to stop him."

This was the first time Charmaine had talked to me about her sexuality. I was glad she was opening up but didn't know quite how to respond. My mind went to Tony and how I wished he had opened up with me. The only thing I could think to say to Charmaine was what Grandmama Pearl always said to me: to be yourself, anyone uncomfortable with that wasn't worth being in your orbit.

"Surround yourself with folks who will love you just the way you are," I told her. She seemed satisfied with that, and that was good enough for me.

I switched on the wiper blades as the rain began to fall. I didn't recall rain in the forecast, and my worst fear came true as it began to turn to sleet. The last thing I wanted was to be on the freeway at night in the middle of an Illinois snowstorm. The tires on the Monte Carlo had long since lost their grove, but I put the pedal to the metal trying to make it home. The slippery freeway could make the road trip a disaster, so I eased off the pedal just as a cloud of smoke rose from under the hood and the car clanked to a slow roll forcing me over to the shoulder as the engine sputtered before coming to a complete stop. Sleet pelted the windshield as the grey sky turned to night and taillights from other cars whizzed past me.

"What the—" I cranked the key and pumped the gas pedal, but the engine screeched louder with each turn. In my rearview window, approaching bright lights illuminated the inside of my car as huge headlamps came to a stop inches from my bumper. The driver side of the eighteen-wheeler swung open and I stiffened as man hopped from the cab and walked toward my window.

"What's the matter?" he yelled as I pumped the gas pedal, causing the engine to screech. "Don't do that, you'll flood it. Pop the trunk." He lifted the hood of a flimsy jacket over his dirty blond hair to shield himself from the freezing rain.

Rattled, but out of options, I popped the trunk and he disappeared into the engine before returning to the window. "Your thermostat went out. Gonna have to replace it. There's an auto part store at the next exit. Get in; I'll drive us."

Every part of my being refused this offer. It had been just a few short years since the Atlanta Murders, and I wasn't convinced they convicted the right man. It was Georgia after all, and you couldn't tell me white folks weren't behind the senseless killings of all of those black boys. There was no way I was getting in this man's truck. I yelled through the rolled-up window, "That's ok, thank you."

"This car ain't moving until that thermostat is replaced, and it's fixing to be a snowstorm out here. I don't mean you no harm. Only trying to help."

I gave him my best black girl stare down.

"How about I give you my driver's license. Leave it in the car with a note. You got a pen, something to write with?" he asked.

He took his driver's license out of his wallet, and I rolled down the window just enough to let him slide it in. It looked like him. His name was Ralph Anderson, and he had an Illinois address.

"Too dangerous to sit in the car and wait. Some fool come along and slam into the back of you going sixty miles an hour on this ice. You don't want that. We'll pick up the thermostat and come right back to install it."

He made sense, and what other option did I have. I opened the glove box and wrote a note on a small writing tablet. *'My car broke down, I'm Sinclair Ellis, and this man, Ralph Anderson, stopped in his 18-wheeler to help. If I go missing, he did it.'*

I climbed out of the car and followed Ralph to his truck hoisting myself up into the seat of the cab where I scoped out my surroundings. My body stiffened at the sight of a mattress laid out in the back seat. I knew immediately I had made the mistake of my life and grabbed the door handle throwing my body against it, but the door had locked behind me. I was about to go ballistic, sheer terror in my eyes as they locked-on Ralph.

Ralph looked at the mattress, then back at me. "I'm on the road a lot, always worried about my wife. If she broke down, would someone stop and help her." He cranked up his engine and pulled the truck onto the freeway.

For a slight minute, a calm washed over me. I heard Grandmama Pearl's voice say, "All white people ain't bad people. Don't judge books by they cover."

He pulled the massive truck off the exit and down a two-lane road stopping in front of an auto shop. Ralph took charge, giving the clerk the make and model of the vehicle and requesting the part he needed. I pulled out the cash and paid for the item as the clerk looked on curiously at my auto shop companion and me. We climbed back into Ralph's truck and headed back to my car.

"Where you headed?" Ralph asked.

"Chicago?"

"From there originally?" he asked, continuing his small talk.

"No. Gary."

"I'm from Georgia myself. Small town outside Atlanta."

I suddenly felt uncomfortable again. I looked over at Ralph, trying to search his eyes for his real intentions. Would he have driven me to the auto supply store if he intended to kill me? "Atlanta? I've never been there. It's been on the news a lot..." My voice trailed off. Not a good time to discuss a serial killer.

Ralph must have sensed my uneasiness. "My wife's a school teacher. She loves her students. Lots of 'em get bused in. Yes, sir, she loves every one of them."

He pulled up behind the Monte Carlo, reached back by the mattress, and grabbed a flashlight. "I'm a need your keys," he said.

"I can hold the flashlight," I said, digging in the bag for my keys.

"I got it." Ralph hopped out and disappeared under the hood of the Monte Carlo. The sleet and rain swished past the headlamps fast and steady now and the temperature was dropping by the minute. It was completely dark, and he propped the flashlight on the engine as he went to work.

I sat in the warm cab, grateful for the help. Since leaving Kahn, living through Tony's trial, purchasing the fourplex and planning our wedding, I'd made little time for church or praying, and was feeling lost. I made a mental note to get back to church or at least pick up my Bible or get down on my knees and thank God for the blessings. Even though I was still a bit nervous, I felt that Ralph was truly a Godsend. Where would I be right now if he hadn't come along when he did? Ralph walked back to the truck, and I said a silent prayer, happy to be on my way.

Ralph jumped in, rubbing his palms together and blowing into his cold hands as he placed them in front of the heat vent. "I ain't got the right tools," he said. "House ain't far from here. We can head there, get my toolbox, then come back."

This roller coaster ride of discomfort was more than I could take. I contemplated my next move. "We can buy it from the auto supply. I have more cash," I said, trying to sound calm.

Ralph didn't look at me. He steered his truck onto the freeway. "It ain't far," he said.

I said the Lord's Prayer silently to myself, hoping to settle my nerves. For the first time during this ordeal, I thought of Danny. If I got out of this alive, I would listen more to his suggestions. He tried to convince me to buy a new car. Had even offered to go with me to avoid the used car salesman experience as a single female. My tunnel vision only had the fourplex in my scope. A new car could wait. My decision the basis for another argument between us, so the last thing I wanted to hear was him telling me, I told you so. I secretly hoped that the stress brought on by the wedding planning and apartment rehab would dissipate once behind us. A piece of me often wondered if I was doing the right thing. Danny didn't seem to be the same person I met in that hospital bed after my attack. Since Carla showed up, a different side of him was revealed.

I stared out of the window, thinking about Danny and me, as Ralph pulled into a quiet bedroom community with neatly manicured lawns. The truck rolled slowly to a stop in front of a two-story brick house with a pick-up truck in the driveway.

"That didn't take too long? Did it?" Ralph said, not waiting on an answer as he got out of the cab and walked toward the house.

I followed him up the walk way between ice covered hedges toward the home where a macramé owl greeted us at the front door. When he put the key in the lock, a woman opened the door and smiled at him, her smile constant as she took me in. She hugged Ralph and reached out her hand to me.

"Hello," the woman said as I shook her hand.

Ralph sat on a bench by the door. "Her car broke down on the freeway," he said unlacing his boots. "Tried fixing it, but gotta get my tools and go back." He pulled off his boots and slid into a pair of house shoes waiting there for him, before shuffling to the back of the house.

"I'm Janie," she said, gesturing me into the living room. "Would you like some tea?" She asked.

"I'm Sinclair. Thank you. That sounds nice."

I was surprised by the ease of acceptance from Janie. Was she used to her husband bringing home stray women? Were they in some kind of fetish cult? Where did Ralph disappear to, anyway? I looked around at the well-decorated home. Photos of Janie and Ralph lined the mantel above the fireplace. It was cozy and inviting, with a strong pride of ownership and the feeling of two people who spoke each other's language. There wasn't a hint of suspicion from Janie. She was warm and accommodating, and I wasn't sure why that made me uneasy.

Janie returned with two mugs of tea on a tray with honey and cream. "I drink it like the Brits," she said. "Try it."

"Was this woman trying to poison me?" I thought. "Trying to knock me unconscious?"

As soon as my suspicion was ramping up, Ralph entered the room wearing a heavier coat, a wool cap, and carrying a toolbox. He sat on the bench neatly placing his slippers back in position and put on his boots. Without conversation between them, Janie grabbed a coat from the closet, and we all headed out to the truck. I was amazed by how in sync with each other they seemed. I became less suspicious as I became more comforted and a little envious of their oneness. He walked over to the pick-up truck in the driveway, opening the front door for Janie, who slid into the middle and me as I slid in behind her. She rested her hand on his knee as they made their way toward the freeway. I stole looks out of the corner of my eye, watching as Ralph gently caressed Janie's hand while he maneuvered the truck with the other. The two of them made me think of my parents and how my father always doted on my mother.

My father, Callen Ellis, made us feel like we were the center of his world. A terrible car crash took him away from us too soon, but he left an impression on me that I'd never forgotten. I was only eight the night news came about his death, but the scream I heard from the front of the house was forever etched in my memory. My mother's piercing cry rocked me from my dreams and snatched me from my bed. I ran toward her anguished cry to find her sprawled on the floor in her nightgown as two police officers stood over her. The indifference on their faces juxtaposed my mother's agony.

The lady officer leaned down to me. "Is there a relative you can call?" she asked.

"Daddy. I want my daddy. He always knows how to calm mommy down," I cried.

The police officer looked back at her partner, who shrugged in indifference. "Is there anyone else, an auntie or uncle?"

I took the officer's hand, led her to the phone on the kitchen wall, and pointed to a list of numbers sprawled on the tablet next to it. In big red letters was written, 'in case of emergency, call Ervin and Mattie Ellis. The officer dialed the number, and the next thing I remember was Aunt Mattie lifting me from the floor, where I sat next to mama, gently stroking her hair. She had stopped screaming and had curled herself in a fetal position on the floor. Aunt Mattie picked me up and I screamed and reached out for my mama while Uncle Ervin talked to the police.

I didn't exactly know when it registered that my father was never coming back again. For years I fantasized about him coming through the door, with my mother by his side and the three of us living together again, but that day never came. All I was left with were the fond memories of how daddy treated momma with so much love and reverence, and I longed for the same.

As the sleet began to turn to snowflakes, I wondered if Danny was the vision of that love. This struck me deep in my soul as I watched Ralph squeeze Janie's hand before hopping out of the truck into the snow to fix my car. Ralph's calm, helpful demeanor reminded me of my father, and for the first time in a long time, I longed for him again.

"Are you from Chicago?" Janie asked, shaking me out of my thoughts.

I looked at Janie, noticing for the first time her vivid brown eyes that seemed to sparkle when she talked. She wore her brunette hair shoulder length with a side-swept bang across her heart-shaped face. Her welcoming smile and soft, delicate voice complimented Ralph's genuine kindness.

"I really appreciate all that you and your husband are going through," I blurted out. "I mean, it's so cold, and he's—"

"He's always worried that something like this might happen to me while he's on the road. Thank God he came along when he did. Had you been stranded long?"

"I'd just pulled over. He must have been right behind me. I was lucky he was there."

"Blessed is more like it. Just one of the many angels God places in our path," Janie said, smiling at me.

I looked at her and nodded. It was like Grandmama Pearl had just spoken to me from the grave. It's exactly something she would say, and I knew Janie was right. She and Ralph were indeed my angels bringing more than one lesson to me on this cold winter night.

Ralph raised his head from under the hood, "Come on and give her a try," he yelled.

I looked into Janie's eyes, slightly choked up, but pushed my emotions aside. "Thank you so much for your kindness," I said.

"We'll follow you into Chicago. Make sure you get back safe." Janie smiled back as I hopped out into the cold night air.

I turned the key and gently patted the gas as the engine turned over without a hitch. I rolled down the window. "Thanks so much, Ralph," I said, handing him back his driver's license.

Ralph took the license and nodded. "We'll follow you a bit. Make sure you get home safe."

Ralph and Janie's identical thoughts not surprising to me. Theirs was the kind of synergy and love mom and dad had. I deserved that, too.

I made my way to my apartment, stepping over the boxes Charmaine had helped pack in preparation for moving to the fourplex. I stripped off my shoes and clothes and stepped into the shower, letting the water caress my tired muscles, then made my way to the kitchen to fix a hot cup of tea.

The flashing light on the answering machine caught my eye. I'd been gone all day and hadn't told anyone where I was. After the day I had, I wasn't up to answering questions or hearing opinions about my visiting Tony.

I shifted around boxes, clearing a seat near the window, and sat and watched the snowflakes drift gently from the sky. Catching my reflection in the window, I gazed back at my image. I couldn't get Ralph and Janie's love connection out of my mind; the intuitive way they seemed to know what the other was feeling was the kind of love language my parents had. I sipped my tea and sighed deeply. Every practical bone in my body knew there were changes in my life that I needed to make, but the emotional side resisted the turmoil those changes would bring.

CHAPTER 10

Danny poured the cognac into his glass and threw it back in one gulp. He let the liquid sting the back of his throat as he poured himself another. He looked out over the icy city. The sleet was coming down steady now, and the city lights illuminated the icy rain as it swished past his window.

He'd just rested on a sex trafficking case and the cognac helped erase the disturbing images burned into his brain. He still hadn't gotten used to the horrid crimes inflicted upon people by other human beings. Carla hadn't raised him in church, but she taught him right from wrong, and the crimes disturbed him deep in his soul. Her rigid schedule of school and work reserved Sundays for catching up on sleep and studying. Their long hours spent in the library surrounded him with books filled with a world of endless discoveries. He was most drawn to the history section, where he absorbed the stories of the American oligarchs who acquired their wealth on the backs of the enslaved Africans they imported to these shores to trade like merchandise and increase their profit and wealth. Slavery, Jim Crow, and the prison industrial complex were lessons that propelled Danny to become a lawyer, to change the imbalance the justice system was designed to protect.

He poured himself another drink, sat in the leather chair behind his desk, picked up the phone and dialed Sinclair, again. He got her answering machine and hung up. He'd already left three messages. He hated it when she wasn't available when he needed her. He'd had a hard day and needed her to make him feel better. It didn't dawn on him to seek his peace within. A lesson the churchless Sunday mornings hadn't taught him, as Sundays spent in church had taught Sinclair.

The phone rang, and he snatched it up, "Hello." He sighed, hearing the voice on the other end. "Oh, hey, Mom."

"Daniel, good evening, son. Why so gloom?"

Danny gulped his drink. "Trial stuff. What's up?"

"I know you think your mind is made up, but I've been speaking to Winston Collier, the campaign manager you were scheduled to meet with—"

"Mom, seriously? I've been over this a thousand times. It's over—"

"Just hear me out," Carla said. "I think you'll find this quite interesting. Winston has received some inside information that Alderman Melvin Tanner's office is about to be raided by the FBI."

Danny sat up straight in his leather chair, "Go on."

"Seems he's been under investigation for bribery charges in exchange for directing funding to several contractors in the city."

Danny tapped a cigarette from its pack. "No news there. They don't call it the windy city because of the weather forecast," he said, looking for matches.

"Sure, it's typical Chicago politics, but he obviously pissed somebody off. Didn't grease the right palms, so they're about to make an example out of him."

"And I care, because?" Danny said, the unlit cigarette dangling from his lips.

"Son, read the writing on the wall. If Tanner is indicted, he won't be able to complete his term. You live in his district, and the city council will have to appoint someone to his seat, and—"

Danny sighed. "I see where this is going, and the answer is still no."

Carla didn't get to where she was in life by giving up easily. She had to fight for everything she ever wanted, and she knew what was best for her son.

"No campaigning, no fundraising, but a heck of a lot of publicity that will position you for that District Attorney run. That's your goal, right? This will sure as hell beat starting from scratch to get there. Look, you're a junior prosecutor. No one knows who you are. You know how Chicago politics are, you run for DA with no heat behind you and you'll fail."

"Thanks for the vote of confidence, Mom."

"Son, I raised you. No one has more confidence in you than me. But I'm also the one that's going to give it to you straight, no chaser. You want a fast track to DA, this is it. Your name plastered in the press as the man who saved the day when Melvin Tanner nearly lost the Ward to a gentrifier. In eighteen months, when DA elections come along, you'll be all anybody is talking about. Let's face it, people vote for names they're familiar with."

Danny let his mother's words pour over him. She always did have a way of making the most outlandish ideas make sense. It was her who told him he could go from cop to the top law school in the country. Growing up, she was always in his ear, telling him that he could be anything he wanted to be if he put his mind to it, and Danny believed her.

"It's all just hypothetical, right now. This Winston guy sounds like no more than the town gossip," Danny said.

"His sources are pretty reliable. Think about it, son. We'll want to be ready when the indictment hits the press. Winston's prepared to launch a campaign to call for Tanner's suspension and recommend you for the seat—the young prosecutor who lives in the same ward. We'll ride the coattails of your inside trader win and have you appointed to that seat in the press before the city council knows what hit them."

Danny looked around his office. A stack of files filed with more horrid crimes awaited his attention. Stepping away from his prosecutor seat for eighteen months with the chance of becoming Chicago's DA didn't seem like a bad move. It sure beat the four-year Alderman term they were initially considering. That sounded reasonable, and he saw no reason why Sinclair couldn't get behind that.

"I'll talk it over with Sinclair."

Silence followed by a long sigh filled the phone line. "Of course, because she's always been so supportive." Carla finally said not hiding her sarcasm. "Talk soon."

The dial tone and the sting of Carla's parting words, buzzed in Danny's ear. Out his window, he saw that the sleet had turned to snow, covering the street below in white powder. The roads would be a mess until street services rolled the salt trucks to clear the way for the morning traffic. As Alderman, maybe he could do something about his neighborhood always being the last to get the service. He picked up the phone again and let it ring for what seemed like several minutes. He lit his cigarette, a nasty habit he thought he'd left behind at law school. What on earth could Sinclair be doing out in this weather. Where had she been all day, and why hadn't she called him back? He grabbed his coat and headed out the door to find out.

CHAPTER 11

I helped mama clean up the mess in the kitchen. She was trying to cook dinner for daddy before he came home from work. I ran and got the broom. "I got it, mama," I said. "I can help." The broom handle towered over me as I tried to get enough leverage to sweep up the cornmeal spilled all over the floor.

Mama stood by the sink, wringing her hands and looking around at the mess she'd made. Butter melted down the front of the stove in a gooey mess; the oven door was open, revealing a pan of burnt cornbread. "Turn it off, Sinclair," she said, pointing at the pot of greens boiling over on the stove. "Damn, Damn!" Mama wailed.

"But, Mama, I can't. Daddy told me don't touch the stove. I'll get burned up, he said—"

"Turn it off," she yelled, squeezing her head between her hands.

The pot bubbled up on the stove escaping steam that drifted through the kitchen. Daddy had told mama not to fuss with big meals during the week. Just wait to Sunday dinners, he told her, when she and Aunt Mattie shared the cooking duties for our big family dinners with daddy and his brothers, Ervin, Ely and Coltrane. Aunt Mattie was married to Uncle Ervin, and Ely and Coltrane would bring whatever girlfriend they had at the moment. They were careful about who they invited cause

Grandmama Pearl had no filter and would tell them exactly what she thought if she felt them to be trifling. Jasmine, Kyle and I played outside with the other kids in the neighborhood before supper. My favorite day of the week was Sundays after church with my family.

I held onto the broom with one hand and made my way over to the stove. It was a brand-new O'Keefe and Merritt with six eyes and two ovens. Daddy had bought it for Mama a few Christmases ago cause she loved to cook. Still, even at seven years old, I could see she wasn't very good at it, but Daddy did anything for mama. I enjoyed watching how much they loved on each other. I held my breath as I stood away from the stove and leaned in to turn off the burner under the greens.

"Got it," I said as the pot ceased its rumbling.

"I'm a go lie down, baby. Mama's got one of her headaches," Mama said.

"But mama, we got to clean up this mess. Daddy be home soon."

"Not right now, Sinclair." Mama lit a cigarette and sat down at the kitchen table. Her hands shook as she lifted the filter to her mouth and took a deep puff. The smoke escaped her lips and she looked around the storm that had blown through her kitchen, watching as my tiny frame tried to maneuver the broom and dustpan to collect the trash, holding them at the same time as I had seen her do.

"Help me, mama," I said, but was startled by the wailing sound that rose from the pit of her stomach. I dropped the broom and ran to her. "Don't cry, mama." She grabbed me, lifted me into her lap, and cried tears into my pigtails, squeezing me tight. I don't how long we sat there, mama crying into my hair like that, but the next thing I heard was banging. It was like it was in the distance and got louder and louder—

Bang, bang, bang, I awoke to my name being called and banging at the door. I'd fallen asleep in the kitchen. I peeled open my eyes and a blanket of snow came into view. It covered the city in a white hallow and for a minute, I felt a peace beyond understanding.

I emerged from my fog and remembered the dream. It had been a long time since I had dreamt of Mama.

Bang, Bang—

I rose from my seat, jockeying around boxes to the front door. I peered through the peephole and opened the door. "What's up?" I said.

Danny raced into the room, "Where you been? I've been calling you all day," he yelled, barging past me down the hall, looking into the bedroom and bath before turning on his heels and marching toward the kitchen.

"What are you looking for?" I asked, cautioned that jealousy and control were other bad personality traits emerging.

"You need to let me know where you are. What's up with disappearing all day like that? I needed you," he said, wailing his arms around and pacing the floor like a caged animal.

Maybe I should have taken a pause. Stood silent and contemplated what would come out of my mouth next. But half asleep, I wasn't thinking as clearly as I could have. "Well, excuse me if my world doesn't revolve around Danny Boone's needs," I said with all of the attitude intact.

He spun around and looked at me like I was a hostile witness. He took a moment before shaking his head at me and saying, "You're so damn selfish, Sinclair. I was worried about you—"

"Were you? Or were you just mad because you needed something, and I wasn't at your beck and call"

"I'm sorry. I didn't know it was a crime for a man to want his woman to be there for him."

"Do you hear yourself right now? You come in here, yelling and talking to me out the side of your neck, talking about what you need."

"Side of my neck," He reared back and laughed. "You should

do something about that wild imagination of yours. I simply responded to the lack of care you showed by disappearing all day and not letting me know where you were."

"Don't pull that lawyer talk on me," I said, "You wouldn't care where I was if you didn't need me. Half the time, you're giving me the damn silent treatment," I said, in his face now, neck rolling. "You're so self-absorbed these days—"

"I'm self-absorbed? Between your wanna-be house flipping escapades, that homeless dike you picked up off the street, and wedding—"

I screamed back at him, "You're a bully! You're so insecure that you take it out on other people because they're comfortable in their own skin. Your mother screwed you around with her high and mighty—"

Danny charged at me, nostrils flaring and his eyes bulging as he stuck his finger in my face, "Don't talk about my mother. You wish you were half the woman she was. At least she's not out here making dumb decisions like quitting a steady job to pursue something she knows nothing about. She's planning ahead, thinking about how she can make our lives better, coming up with a way for me to fast track my DA goals."

I found this amusing. "Yeah, right with a four-year trip through hell and back in some thankless Alderman's job. Way to plan ahead. I guess that's one idea we both agreed was dumb."

Danny shrugged. "May not have to run for it or serve four years. Mom found a way around it."

This hit me like a brick. My stomach twisted into a knot big enough to anchor a cruise ship as a life that included Carla flashed before my eyes. I looked at Danny like his head screwed on and off. My uneasiness not enough to stop him from saying another word about Carla.

"Mom thinks I can get appointed to finish out Tanner's seat," he said.

"Tanner's seat?" I was trying to make sense of the nonsense coming out of his mouth.

"Looks like the feds have him in their sites. I can ride out his term for the next eighteen months, then run in the next election for the DA seat. Alderman appointment will give me the heat I need to win."

The room fell silent as I took a moment to gather myself. That's what this was about. Why he charged over here talking about needing me. He was there to try and justify Carla's bullshit! At that moment, I knew she would forever be in the middle of our lives—just like she manipulated herself between us the first day I met her.

I looked at Danny in disbelief. We had hashed this out. Any form of being an Alderman in this city could not end well. Melvin Tanner's ward was the most toxic in the city, and the vultures would come at Danny like fresh meat.

I sat down on the couch, "What makes you think they'll appoint you?" I said.

"Mom and the campaign manager she wants to introduce me to have a plan."

"We talked about this, Danny." Visions of the sweet, thoughtful man I'd met in my hospital room that day had disappeared, and I knew at that moment he was gone for good. Danny had changed; his hunger for a power that was being impinged upon him by Carla had distorted his soul.

Danny moved a box out of the way and sat down next to me. He took a cigarette out of a pack and looked around for matches.

"You're smoking, again?" I asked.

"It got me through the trial," he said, striking the match and aiming smoke to the ceiling.

His need for a crutch was something I hadn't noticed before. "Try prayer," I heard myself say.

We'd talked about going to church together. While Danny had never attended, I was raised going to church every Sunday, and we agreed we'd raise our children that way, too. His comment about my leaving a steady income to pursue my real estate investment goals had hit hard. We'd spoken about how my faith played a big part in my decision. He had told me he supported me, but ever since I started the apartment rehab, his criticism had become more and more telling.

"That's your thing. For me, I'm going to bet on myself, not some blue-eyed white boy that's got the world convinced he can pull magic out of a hat."

I looked at him like he had grown a tail. "We agreed that we'd raise our kids in church."

"We did. Didn't say I was going, though, did I?"

"I understood that to be the case. I was clear that it was what I wanted for our family."

"What you wanted. Look, raise the kids in church. Besides, with the DA gig, I'll be so busy, Sundays will be reserved for rest, relaxation, and maybe viewing a few briefs. Like Mom and I did when I grew up."

You could cut the silence with a knife. We sat there in our own thoughts for what seemed like an eternity. He finished his smoke and extinguished it in a cup of soda that Charmaine had left from her fast-food meal. It made me think of her honesty about who she was and what she wanted. I took a page from her playbook. I sighed deeply, exhaling any doubt that what I was about to do wasn't the best thing for us both.

I didn't look at him. I just stared straight ahead at the boxes around the room, signifying my next chapter in life. It was crystal clear to me now what Grandmama Pearl meant by finding someone who was equally yoked. I blew it off before, but it had just blown back and smacked me in the face. Two people on the opposite ends of faith, would eventually be pulled in different directions. I felt it best if Danny and I did it now rather than later. "We'll lose the deposit on the venue and dress," I said, feeling no further need for explanation.

Danny lit another cigarette and looked around the room. "Where's that bottle of cognac," he asked.

I shook my head and shrugged, "Packed, I guess."

He ran his hand through his hair, "So, it's like that?"

"I think we both know it is."

He reached for me and I pulled away.

"I can't change your mind," he said.

I shook my head.

"Mom paid for the band in full. She'll be pissed she can't get her money back."

Carla was the last person I wanted to talk about right now. "She'll be alright."

I stood up, walked to the door and opened it. I didn't look at him. I didn't want to look into his eyes and see the pain I was feeling staring back at me. He took what seemed like forever to get up and move toward the door. When he did, he stopped in front of me, stood there and rested his chin on my bowed head. He kissed my crown and stepped over the threshold into the hall.

I shut the door behind him resting my palm on the back of the door, steadying myself. There were no tears, just a deep sadness that engulfed me like an itchy blanket. I went to the couch and curled up in a ball, trying to wrap my mind around how the decision to walk away from the man I'd plan to spend the rest of my life with, came with such ease and pain at the same time.

CHAPTER 12

Jasmine rolled her car to the curb and before she could come to a stop, Tina was already opening the passenger door.

"Hold up, girl. Let me park the car," Jasmine said.

Charmaine walked toward them as Jasmine put the car in park. "She won't open the door?" She said, her voice trembling.

"Or answer her phone. I've been calling for a week," Tina said, hopping out of the car. She gave Charmaine a hug. "It's ok," she whispered.

Jasmine joined Tina and Charmaine on the sidewalk, "Has anyone heard from Danny?"

Charmaine and Tina shrugged, "Called him several times," Charmaine said, "but then I'm the last person he'll take a call from."

"Well, hopefully, they're just laid up in here doing the nasty all week," Jasmine said, walking toward the door.

"Then she needs to let a sistah know," Tina said, following Jasmine to the door.

Jasmine used her key to let them into the lobby. Sinclair had given her a key when she kited that check and moved into the high rise a few short years ago. This was the first time Jasmine had to use it and was glad she had it. As kids growing up, their families always had the keys to each other's homes, and they continued that tradition when they got out on their own and moved from Gary to Chicago.

They all marched to the elevator on a mission and rode up in silence. They didn't know what to expect when they reached her apartment. Tina thought about the first time she'd visited Sinclair's apartment. She was there helping her cousin move into the building and remembered Sinclair had told her she lived there. They weren't even friends then. They both worked at Kahn Telecommunications, and Tina was actually hating on Sinclair, jealous about Sinclair's pending promotion. She gazed up at the elevator buttons as they blinked toward Sinclair's floor. They'd come a long way, from co-worker rivalry to the friendship they had now. Tina's heart fluttered at the thought of finding Sinclair anything but safe and sound in her apartment, snuggled up with Danny. Why wasn't she answering the phone? Sinclair wouldn't leave them hanging like that.

They stepped out of the elevator, and the trio made their way down the hall like Charlie's Angels on a mission.

Charmaine knocked. "Sinclair! It's us. Open up."

Jasmine put her ear to the door, listening for signs of life. Thoughts of Violet Ellis, Sinclair's mother, and her struggle with mental illness played out in her mind, and a terrible wave rushed over her. She side-stepped Charmaine and banged on the door in a frantic fit.

"Sinclair! Sin! It's me! It's Jasmine. Are you in there? Open the door, sweetie, please! Let us in," Jasmine pleaded. "Please let us in."

Suddenly, they heard the door lock click. They all fell silent as Sinclair cracked the door and peered out at them. "Hey. What's up?" she said out of one side of her face pressed against the door, trying to shield her bloodshot eyes.

Tina threw up her hands. "What's up?! You, what's up. Been trying to reach you for a week. What the—"

Jasmine gestured for Tina to chill. "Hey, Sin. We've been worried about you. What's going on? Let us in." They were like sisters. They'd grown up together in the same duplex since they were kids and had been thick as thieves ever since. Jasmine knew when she was hurting and knew that it took a tragedy of monumental extreme to knock Sinclair down, and right now, she was looking down for the count.

Sinclair stepped aside and let her friends in. They were met with the moving boxes strewn about the room, half-eaten take-out bags, and an empty bottle of cognac. They entered the room and looked around at the mess. It had been almost a week since Danny and Sinclair broke off the wedding and she hadn't moved far from the couch where she had curled herself into a ball after he left. Hadn't called anyone, spoken to anyone, or even taken a shower.

Tina turned up her nose, "What died in here?"

Jasmine jabbed her with her elbow.

Sinclair flopped down on the couch. "Just go away," she said, covering her head in a blanket.

The women looked at each other, unsure what to do next. Jasmine took charge, motioning to Tina and Charmaine, who followed her cue. Tina headed for the bathroom as Charmaine cleared the week-old take-out and cracked the window to air the place out.

Jasmine went to Sinclair's side. "What's the matter, Sin? What happened? Talk to me."

"I just keep messing up," she moaned from beneath the blanket before erupting into uncontrollable sobs.

Jasmine held her tightly, then slowly lifted her to a seated position. "Come on, sweetie. Let's get you a hot shower. You'll feel better, then you can tell us all about it." She rose to her feet. Bent and sobbing,

Sinclair rose with her and managed one foot in front of the other as her cousin led her to the bathroom, where Tina had started the shower. They peeled off her week-old clothes and helped her into the tub. The water flowed over Sinclair's matted hair and drenched her body.

Jasmine helped her shampoo and wash. She was reminded of the baths they took together as children. Giggling and playing in the tub with barbie dolls before Aunt Mattie would come in and lather them up and shampoo their hair. The last time she saw Sinclair so distraught was the night Aunt Mattie brought her home when they got the news that her father had been killed in an accident. The rumors in the neighborhood were that Callen Ellis had a woman in Chicago that had his child. When he tried to break it off, she lost her mind and threatened to take her and the baby's life. He grabbed the child and ran out to his truck. When she ran out and jumped in front of him as he tried to speed away, he swirled to avoid hitting her and rammed the truck into a tree, killing himself and the child. Sinclair lost her mother and father that day, and a half baby brother, she would never know. Her mother, fragile by an already worsening mental illness, had a breakdown she never returned from and was institutionalized. That's when Sinclair came to live in the duplex, across the hall from Jasmine, her brother, Kyle, and their family. Jasmine's mother and Aunt Mattie were sisters. Mattie and Ervin Ellis, Callens brother, raised Sinclair from that day forward. Even though she and Jasmine weren't blood cousins, they were inseparable, then and now.

Jasmine wrapped a towel around Sinclair and helped her out of the shower. She toweled dried her hair as Sinclair sat on the toilet and let her cousin take care of her. Jasmine helped her put on her robe, and the two joined Tina and Charmaine at the dining room table. They sat among the boxes as Sinclair told them that her wedding was canceled and her marriage to Danny would not be.

"This is not what I was expecting. I mean, I didn't know what to expect, but this certainly wasn't it," Charmaine said.

"I need to cancel everything... Oh my God. The invitations. They've—"

Tina put her arm around Sinclair, "Don't worry. We're here. How do you want us to help?"

Jasmine had sat silently during Sinclair's blow by blow of the whole ordeal. She was watching Sinclair's body language as much as she was listening to her words. She felt her pain and the isolation Sinclair chose instead of turning to her friends. "Wait! Are you sure it's over? Maybe you can reconcile this before we go canceling all the work you put into this wedding."

Exacerbated, Sinclair pushed away from the table. "It's better than putting work into a marriage destined to fail," Sinclair said.

Charmaine nodded her agreement. "She's got a point there."

Jasmine wasn't convinced. "It can't be over, just like that."

Sinclair walked to the window and looked out. The fresh snowfall that occurred the night of her break-up was now mounds of brown slush and ice pushed to the side of the road. Her life with Danny had started off like freshly fallen snow. Their love, fresh and pure for one another, now pushed to the side of the road, derailed, never to get back on track again. She laid in that apartment for practically a week feeling sorry for herself. Beating herself up for missing what became so obvious to her. She wasn't marrying Danny; it was Trace all along. She'd conjured up this fantasy that Trace would somehow be in her life forever and turned Danny into more than the chance meeting that it was. During that week, she'd thought of all her failures, blaming herself for everything from her abuse from Uncle Ervin to Yusef Green, her employment struggles after college, to her struggles with her contractor from hell. She'd laid there in a pool of pity for the last week, convinced that she was a total hot mess. But, thanks to her friends who rescued her from her pity pit, she was gaining her strength. She knew she wasn't to blame for any of it and decided then and there to take her power back.

Sinclair turned to her friends, "It's over!" She took a deep breath and surveyed the apartment, the boxes, and yet-to-be-packed items strewn about. "Y'all want to help? Let's get to packing. There's a truck scheduled to arrive in a few days to move me into my new life."

Tina hopped up from her seat. "There she is. That's my girl."

Jasmine smiled. They all stood and embraced in a group hug.

Charmaine broke the moment, "I didn't like his ass, anyway."

They had a good laugh and got to work!

CHAPTER 13

Like everything dealing with the four-plex, the rehab on the other three units took longer than anticipated. Melvin, the contractor from hell, had to be replaced. Once he learned that Danny was no longer around, he thought my head screwed on and off and attempted crazy shortcuts to get the work done.

I interviewed a dozen contractors before Leon, my loan officer, referred me to a brother and sister, El Salvadorian immigrants, who were getting their new construction business off the ground. She served as the project manager and he ran the crews who did the work—exactly as planned. When we encountered some unexpected issues, dealing with Luisa was a breath of fresh air behind Melvin. Even her brother, Carlos, was respectful and accommodating. He was tall with coal-black eyes and a curly head of hair that fell just past his chiseled chin. I kept my flirting in tack. A man was the last thing I wanted to get entangled with. I hadn't seen or spoken with Danny since he walked out of my apartment that day, but the rumors were rampant about a possible indictment of Alderman Tanner. I drowned out that noise and anything else to do with Danny.

I was standing outside, peering through a hole in the ground where Carlos was shining his flashlight.

"Pipe rusted," he said, shining his light at a huge pipe. "Main line needs fix," he revealed as best he could in his broken English.

I looked into those black pearl eyes, "How much?"

He stared down into the hole and scratched his head beneath his Chicago Bulls cap. "Oh, I don't know. Luisa tell you. She come later."

Fixing a plumbing problem wasn't in the budget. I'd allocated the money received from the investments Tony made to the penny. I had calculated a small margin for error when deciding to quit my job at Kahn after working with Gloria became unbearable, but cash flow was negative until I flipped the first property. Proceeds from that would lead to the next purchase until, eventually, I'd built enough capital and creditworthiness to invest in major developments. That's where the money was. I'd watched Uncle Ervin manage his apartment buildings throughout Gary. He'd sometimes take Jasmine, Kyle, and me to collect his rent. Watching his tenants duck and dive when they saw him coming wasn't the vision I had for my real estate investments. I was good in math and found myself always adding up his money from all the buildings we visited, and knew one day, real estate investment would be my ticket to freedom, and major developments—not apartment buildings—would land me in the VIP section.

I checked my watch. The plumbing problem had set me behind schedule. I said goodbye to Carlos and his crew and ran to my car, another unexpected expense. After Ralph rescued me from the side of the road and fixed the thermostat, the hooptie broke down again. I took some of my savings and paid cash for what the salesman told me was a reliable pre-owned vehicle. I took Jasmine, Tina and Charmaine with me to the dealership. I figured between the four of us, a salesperson would think twice about selling me a lemon.

"It got a warranty?" Charmaine asked. She towered over the

used car salesman. He had dark black hair slicked back with grease and a cheap suit that shined like silver.

"Pop the hood," Tina demanded and proceeded to stick her head in. The battery cables looked fine to me, but Tina negotiated a brand-new battery.

"Trust me, Sin, the last thing you want is a dead battery in Chicago in the middle of winter,' she said.

We went inside and the silver suite salesman offered us day-old coffee. He quoted a price and played the let-me-ask-my-manager game when I offered him a lower amount. When he returned with a price still higher than we all agreed I should pay, I stood up to leave. "I'm going to look around some more. Go to that lot across the street and see what they got."

Jasmine stood on cue, "They had a cute little Mustang over there," she said as Tina and Charmaine stood up too.

Silver Suit stood up, "Wait a minute, hold on now. Maybe I can convince my manager to give you a better deal. Depends on your credit, though. What's your credit like?"

I chuckled at the salesman. "Cash!" I said.

It wasn't the Mercedes Benz I wanted. Still, an hour later, we were driving off the lot in a used car at the price I negotiated with a brand-new battery and a twelve-month bumper-to-bumper warranty.

I was happy I bought the car today as I cruised down Lakeshore singing out loud to the radio, a luxury I'd missed in the hooptie. I pulled into the garage of McCormick Place, thankful that the parking gods were on my side. I snatched a spot near the entrance and jetted inside.

I dashed through the exhibition hall past a Pharmaceutical Sales convention toward the Arie Crown Center. It was the second-largest theater in Chicago and the site for the Real Estate Investment seminar that I was rushing to get to.

I made my way through the crowd, up the escalator, and past the ballrooms. As I walked, my mind calculated the amount of revenue the massive development pulled in each year for the McCormick family. They'd made their money on the invention of reaper machines, which were said to have helped break the bonds of slavery by mechanizing the harvesting of grain. I smiled as I walked up to the registration desk, picturing myself, a descendent of slaves, owning a development as grand as the McCormick's convention center.

"Sinclair Ellis," I said to the registration attendant as I pulled the registration confirmation from my purse and handed it to her. "I have VIP seats for the seminar for two." I scanned the crowd looking for Charmaine, the only one who had accepted my invitation.

Tina and Jasmine had declined. Jasmine was spending her Saturday with Doc. They were getting pretty close, even though she'd shared they hadn't slept together yet, which she couldn't determine a good or bad sign. Tina was tight-lipped about her plans, and I made a note to get in her business to find out what she'd been up to. She hadn't even had us over since moving to her new apartment, so I knew something was up.

I heard my name called over the chatter of attendees and spun around, expecting to see Charmaine, but looked into the face of Leon, my mortgage loan officer, who had suggested I purchase the fourplex as a first-time homebuyer instead of an investor, and who'd also told me about the real estate investment seminar that day.

"I see you made it," he said, opening his arms for a hug.

"Wouldn't have missed it. It's right up my alley," I said, accepting the embrace.

"This I know. You will be amazed. How's the rehab going?"

I rolled my eyes.

"That bad, huh?"

I shrugged. "It's never a dull moment. Luisa and Carlos are

great. Thanks for the recommendation. They discovered a plumbing problem that's gonna set me back; other than that, everything's peachy."

Leon laughed. "The joy of flipping is so flipping fun."

It wasn't that funny, but I was cracking up when I spotted Charmaine across the room and waved her over. "Leon, this is Charmaine. She's been a big help with the decorating. A regular Black Martha Stuart."

Leon pointed his thumb toward Charmaine and looked at me through one eye, "The squatter?" he asked with no filter.

"Miss Squatter to you," Charmaine said, not missing a beat.

Urged on by her sense of humor, "Welcome Squatter Stuart," Leon said, "to the best real estate investment seminar you'll ever attend. They even have a breakout session on decorating on a budget that you might find interesting."

"Uh, you can call me Charmaine," she said, looking at Leon sideways.

Leon stood at attention, clicked his heels together and saluted, "Yes, ma'am."

People began to file into the theater. "Let's find our seats," I said, "before the VIP section gets crowded."

We made our way into the theater. It wasn't long before the presenter hit the stage. It was a grand entrance with music and lights that made you feel like you were at a concert instead of a real estate seminar. One presenter after the other took the stage and mesmerized the audience with everything from how to use other people's money to invest in deals to how to purchase properties in default at below-market prices. I practically floated out of the auditorium. I was becoming obsessed with my real estate goals and was ready to dive into my next deal.

We were standing in the foyer, viewing the agenda to determine what breakout sessions to attend for the day. "I'ma definitely take advantage of this decorating on a budget," Charmaine said.

"You could probably teach that," I said. "What about you, Leon?"

Leon had stopped behind us. He was talking to a white boy dressed to the nines in an Armani suit. I blinked cause I don't think I've ever seen a white boy in Stacy Adams; he looked like a walking mannequin—the complete opposite of the tracksuits and Jordans men my age were wearing. Not that I didn't admire a great tracksuit, but slightly older men had become my weakness since Trace.

Leon and Armani suit stepped toward us. "Sinclair, let me introduce you to one of my clients. This here is the man. I've brokered several deals for him and about to move into the commercial space. Same as you, eventually."

"Really," I said. "Would love to pick your brain sometime. I'm not there yet, but let's just say I'm inspired. I'm Sinclair. I didn't get your name."

He held out his hand, "What up? Kash Kingsley," he said, "and you can pick my brain anytime, beautiful."

Knocked off guard by the black dialect coming out of this white man's mouth, I stood there holding on to his hand a fraction longer than what was sociable before Charmaine cleared her throat, reeling me back to reality. "Oh, excuse me," I said, dropping his hand and gesturing toward Charmaine. "This is Charmaine."

"Sisters," he asked.

Charmaine huffed. She didn't take too kindly to strangers and held a special disdain for white ones. "Naw, Ken," she said. Then turned to me, "I'ma head to that session, Sin. Let's meet here after. We got that thing with Jas and Tina."

"Got it," I said.

Kash was bemused. "Did she just call me, Ken?"

"She a trip," Leon said.

I cocked my head his way, "She's a teenager. I think I'm going to check out the session on OPM," I said, using the term the speaker used for other people's money.

"Can I hang with you?" Kash asked. "You coming, Leon?" he said, not waiting for my answer.

"Naw, KK man, go on do your thing. Hell, I am other people's money and don't y'all forget about a brother. I got you on that commercial deal," Leon said, pointing back toward Kash and heading to a crowd of people gathering. He whipped out his card and introduced himself. "Leon Lacey, mortgage consultant. I got that OPM y'all looking for."

Kash and I made our way to the breakout session. I took copious notes while he sat at the table, his hands clasped in front of him. Every now and then, he'd either nod or shrug off something the speaker said. When the session was over, I asked him about it.

We'd stopped in the food court and grabbed a quick bite. "I noticed you had some issues with what the speaker was saying," I said.

"You know how it goes. It's all about them tryna sell you something."

"All about them Benjamins," I joked as I handed the cashier money for the food I had purchased.

"On me," Kash said, reaching over me and handing the cashier his American Express.

"Thanks, but you don't have to do that."

Kash insisted, so I acquiesced and found a table. I purposely chose a quiet table in the corner because I really did want to pick his brain and wasn't sure I would ever see him again. We ran in different circles and running into him again may be a long shot.

"So, how long you been in the real estate game?" I asked.

He unwrapped his burger and took a huge bite, shaking his

head with satisfaction. "This ain't half bad for a food court. How's your salad?" he asked, taking another bite of his burger.

"It'll do. Going out with friends later, so saving room for dinner?"

"Where y'all stepping to?"

"Just hanging out. Leon mentioned you were moving into commercial. Shopping center, strip mall?" I realized he hadn't answered my question.

"Commercial, but residential space. Thirty units. More like a mixed-use development deal," he said.

"Oh, apartment buildings." My lack of enthusiasm wasn't lost on him.

"You sound disappointed," he said.

"Tenants. Don't want that hassle."

"You gonna have tenants either way, baby girl," he said, sucking soda through his straw.

"Triple net, though." I was quoting the term I'd just picked up in the OPM session.

Kash laughed. "So, you were paying attention, I see."

I held up my notepad. "Hanging on every word. Didn't see you taking any notes."

"All up here," he said, tapping his finger to his forehead.

"Impressive. Photographic memory?"

"Naw, been there done that," he said, waving a French fry around in the air. What that old white man was talking about ain't nothing new."

I laughed so hard I had to cover my mouth to keep from spitting my salad across the table.

Kash narrowed one eye, "What's so funny?"

"You," I said, trying to quail my laugh. "I've never heard a white man call another white man white. Not like that, anyway—"

Kash looked from side to side as if there was someone else I was talking about. He pointed to his chest—*me?* Then grimaced. "I ain't white!"

I held my laugh this time. He was dead serious. I looked at his face; maybe I missed something. He had thick wavy brown hair and dark grey eyes; he wasn't the palest white person I'd seen, but calling him black was a stretch for me. He did have that unmistakable black dialect, and I couldn't forget them Stacy Adam shoes. Seriously, his outfit was only missing the matching Fedora that was signature to black men's attire.

I realized my mouth was open. "Oh," was all I could muster. "I didn't—"

"You tripping," he said, his feelings clearly hurt. "I don't even believe you went there." He crumbled up his trash, threw it onto the tray, and poked the straw in and out of his drink in an agitated manner.

"I apologize. I can't... I mean, I'm sure other people..." He let me stammer away in my discomfort before he let me off the hook and started cracking up.

Kash was laughing so hard, tears ran down his cheeks. "You should see your face, right now."

I let out a sigh of relief. "I knew it. So, you are a white boy,"

"Hell no. Well, half. The old girl is white. Pops is black; he raised me. So that's what I am in my bones." He leaned into me, "Until I walk up in that bank to get them Benjamins. I let them white boys think what the hell they want if it's going to get me my money."

He was animated and funny, and I found myself leaning into his contagious charisma. "I thought Leon was your boy for that."

"Leon's cool for some things. But I'm going big, baby girl, and when I do, Leon ain't gonna be able to touch that."

"Why not?"

He stretched his arms out, "I'm talking McCormick deals. Them white boys not gonna let Leon broker that kind of money. They want that commission all to themselves. That's how this real estate game works. They may throw him some crumbs if he's lucky."

I let this rush over me. These are things that black folks know instinctively but are told by society that we tripping, pulling the race card. Kash just said it, so matter of fact, it took the wind out of my sails a little. He must have noticed my defeat.

"You'll be alright," he said. "They also like a good money-making deal. At the end of the day, the only color that matters is green. You just gotta have your ducks in a row."

"That's why I'm here," I said, refusing to be discouraged. "Lining them up."

"Oh, I see you," Kash said, giving me his narrowed one-eye look. "With your little notebook and shit."

I checked my watch. "Oh, wow, it's gotten late," I said, getting up. "I've got to go. Thanks so much for the salad. Keep in touch."

"Going to need those digits for that," he said.

I tore a piece of paper from my notebook, scribbled my number, and handed it to him. We wished each other well and headed down the escalator back to the registration desk. I spotted Charmaine through the small crowd still milling about. She folded her arms when she saw me.

"Sorry," I said. "I was getting some good information. That's why we're here, right? How was your session?"

We trekked back past the ballrooms. "Got some good tips to try out. Where did you park?"

"We're almost there," I said as we made our way through the convention halls. I was thinking of Kash and our matching goals of McCormick size developments and was convinced the meeting was a sign that I was on the right track.

CHAPTER 14

J asmine was the first to arrive at the meet-up spot. They picked a neighborhood restaurant by Prairie Shores, a high-rise community not far from McCormick Place. It was a celebration for Tina who had received her acceptance letter from the university. It had been a few months since Sinclair and Danny had broken up and they were also celebrating getting her through it.

Jasmine claimed a table near the jukebox. They liked this spot for casual greetings the jukebox and dart games made for a great way to meet men. Even though she and Doc were seeing a lot of each other, Jasmine always kept her options open.

"What can I get you?" the waitress said, making her way over to Jasmine's table before she could get situated. The other reason they liked that spot—the great service, unlike places where they had to wave the wait staff down.

"Vodka, splash of orange juice," Jasmine said.

"Make that two, only more OJ in mine," Tina said as she walked up to the table.

Jasmine stood and they hugged. "Congratulations. So proud of you."

Tina beamed with joy. "I'm hyped. Thank you and Sinclair for pushing me to do this."

"Girl, that's all Sinclair. She's been nagging you about school since y'all became friends."

"That's what friends are for. Better than nagging me to hit a pipe or something. How's she doing, by the way? She's hard to catch up with these days."

"She good. Had a little mishap with her contractor, but I think that's straight now."

Tina nodded. "Been throwing herself into that real estate stuff."

"Stuff is right. Anything to keep her mind off of you-know-who."

"So, his name's off limits?" Tina said as the waiter brought the drinks.

Jasmine stirred her drink with the cocktail straw. "Would you want to hear his name?" she said, chunking her straw on the table and taking a long sip of her Vodka.

Tina saw Charmaine and Sinclair come through the door and waved them over. "Over here, ladies—" She grimaced. "Oops, do they like to be called ladies?" she asked, looking at Charmaine. "I don't want to offend nobody."

Jasmine gulped the rest of her drink. "What I look like? The lesbian police?" she said, crunching on ice. She made eye contact with the waitress and pointed to her glass for another as Sinclair and Charmaine joined them at the table.

Sinclair handed Tina a gift. It was wrapped in beautiful red paper with a white bow and red and white streamers. She leaned over and gave her friend a hug. "I knew you could do it. You'll be running Kahn Telecommunications before it's over with. Speaking of Kahn, how's Moose and Lincoln, and them?"

Sinclair didn't see much of her ex-coworkers. She'd left Kahn behind and hadn't looked back. She ran into Mason, the manager that promoted her from installation to the studio. He'd told her that Gloria had gotten hired to run a communications company somewhere in Los Angeles. Sinclair was amazed how she could so easily get another executive position after the damage she'd left behind at Kahn. She wondered who in LA she and her icky husband were sexually assaulting now.

"Moose is good; told me to tell you hi," Tina said,

The waiter brought Jasmine's drink and took Charmaine and Sinclair's order. Tina admired her wrapped gift in awe.

"This wrapping paper is so cool. I don't want to unwrap it. You know you love your red. Those were your wedding colors—" She hadn't said his name, but the mention of the wedding was enough to conjure up the painful ordeal. "I'm sorry, I, this is a celebration—"

"No worries. It is from my wedding stuff. I thought I'd purchase a gift for Carla before I realized I was dealing with Mommy-in-law Dearest."

"Hide the hangers!" Jasmine shouted, a little tipsy now.

Sinclair looked at Jasmine's near-empty glass, "Ok, Miss Thing, pace yourself."

"Don't start with me, Sin," Jasmine shouted.

"I'm not—"

"I'm a grown-ass woman. Don't need you counting my cocktails."

Sinclair put her hands up. "Ok, cousin. I'll be here when you need a ride home," she said, trying to make light of the situation and talk Jasmine down.

"I caught the L. Doc's picking me up," Jasmine said, looking over the menu. "I'm ready to eat, y'all ordering?" She blinked, trying to bring the blurry text into focus.

Pointing out Jasmine's drinking was a trigger for her. She didn't see anything wrong with having a few drinks. As hard as she worked and studied, it was the least she could do to treat herself to a little rest and relaxation. She was tired of Sinclair's snide remarks. Just because Jasmine's mother was an alcoholic when they were kids didn't mean that she was anything like her. Her mother drank every day, so much that Jasmine could hardly remember what her mother was like sober. She and Kyle were used to her falling asleep and burning up dinner or forgetting to pick them up from school or practice. Her father never left her, but he was never home either. Kyle said he'd been told their daddy had another family across town. Jasmine didn't know if her mother drank so much because of that or if her father stepped out because of the drinking. She half-believed Kyle anyway until he pointed out a boy at the skating rink where they went as kids who looked just like him and their daddy. She asked Grandmama Pearl if it was true, and even she said it was cheap gossip. Jasmine's mom, Vida, and Aunt Mattie were sisters, and Grandmama Pearl didn't appreciate folks talking trash about her daughters. It was Grandmama Pearl who kept her eye on Jasmine and Kyle when Vida was too drunk to see straight. They spent a lot of time on Aunt Mattie and Uncle Ervin's side of the duplex, especially after Sinclair's mother was committed and Sinclair came to live with them. If it wasn't for Grandmama Pearl looking out for everyone in that duplex, Jasmine was sure Vida's drunk ass would have burnt the house down with all of them in it.

The waitress took their order, and Tina opened her gift. It was a beautiful pen and pencil set with her name engraved in gold letters. She took her time admiring them, turning them over and feeling the weight of them in her hand. She opened the envelope so that the flap wouldn't tear and pulled out the card Sinclair had written in perfect handwriting. As she read it, tears pooled in her eyes.

"This is too much. I've never had friends like y'all. There was always some drama..." she said, sniffling. Tina stopped to catch her breath and suppressed the sobbing that tried to escape from her lips. "Just, always something crazy going on... I... just... thank you, Sinclair, Jasmine, and you too, Charmaine. Thank y'all so much."

"You'll do great. You killed it in junior college, the university is just the next step." Sinclair said.

The waitress arrived with their tray of food and another drink for Jasmine. They ate and chatted, catching up on each other's lives. Sinclair told them about meeting Kash and they had a good laugh about how he busted her out for thinking he was white. She caught them up on the rehab but stopped short of telling them her goals for McCormick size developments. She figured she could show them better than tell them.

Tina wanted to know more about what was up with Doc. "Haven't seen him since the skating rink," she said. How's that going?"

"I can't say. Haven't s... s... slept wit' wit' him yet," Jasmine said.

Tina laughed. She was a romantic; her view of the world was colored by the shows on television. She secretly dreamed of a relationship like Clair and Cliff Huxtable of the Cosby show. "I didn't ask how he screwed. How's getting to know him going?"

Jasmine flailed her hands around. "Ion know if Ion know how he fuck."

Sinclair looked at Charmaine, embarrassed for her. "Ok, guys, we have a minor among us," she said.

"Sh... sh... she ain't, she ain't no, no kid. Proly fucking herself." Jasmine said, her eyes trying to focus in on Charmaine. "Bet ya she don' wan' no dic—"

"Jasmine!! Stop it." Sinclair said, reaching for her glass, "You've had enough."

Jasmine snatched the glass back, spilling vodka down the front of her blouse, "See whatcha did? See, Sinclair?"

Charmaine rose to her feet. "I have to make curfew. I'll talk to you later, Sinclair."

"I was going to drive you back. Give me—"

"I'm good. You got your hands full," Charmaine said. "I'll catch the L." She dug in her bag and pulled out a few crumpled bills.

"Oh, no," Sinclair handed her back the money. "I invited you out for the day. It's on me, and I'm so sorry about… She's had too much to drink; she'd never say things like that sober."

"Naw, but she'd be thinking it. That vodka just gave her courage," Charmaine said, stuffing the money in her bag. "Just like my old man. Crack head or drunk, both pathetic." She slung her bag over her shoulder and walked out.

Jasmine was still glaring at the spilled drink, "You owe me a drink, Sin." She stood up, swaying from side to side. "I be back, gotta pee." She stumbled, grabbing the chair for balance as the room spun around her.

Tina looked at Sinclair. "You going to help her?" she asked.

Sinclair sat with her hands folded. She narrowed her eyes at Jasmine and shook her head.

"Well, somebody has to," Tina got up and stood by Jasmine's side and helped her to the bathroom.

Sinclair picked up her drink to take a sip, looked at the liquor in her glass, and set it back down. Thoughts of Aunt Vida and her own mother circled her brain. Their illnesses were a reminder of the fragility of their minds. She and Jasmine were dealing with the aftermath of discovering they both were abused by Uncle Ervin. Jasmine had convinced Sinclair to go to therapy after the trauma resurfaced in her life from Yusef's attack. Jasmine had already been in therapy, unaware that Sinclair had suffered the same abuse from their uncle. But the years of therapy did little to silence the shame she felt. Her only remedy to cancel out the pain was alcohol.

Sinclair rubbed her temples with her palms and signed deeply. She felt helpless, she wanted to help her cousin, but the first hurdle to accepting help was admitting you needed it, and Jasmine hadn't even come out of the blocks yet.

Sinclair opened her eyes to a tall, handsome man standing at the front of the restaurant, looking around. She recognized him from the skating rink. She glanced toward the bathroom, then back at him as he made his way to the table.

"Sinclair, right?" Jasmine's cousin?" he said in his baritone voice.

Sinclair kept glancing toward the bathroom. "Yes. How are you? Jas will be out in a sec. She's in the lady's room."

He motioned to one of the empty chairs.

"Yeah, yeah, have a seat," Sinclair said.

He folded his large frame into the chair, "I'm Doc; we met at the skating rink."

"I remember."

"Looks like you ladies had a nice dinner," he said, looking at the empty plates still strewn about the table.

Sinclair nodded, "It was interesting."

They sat in awkward silence for a moment. A situation that wouldn't usually bother Sinclair. She was comfortable in her own skin, and silence in her book was golden, but she kept imagining Jasmine stumbling out of the bathroom.

Sinclair shifted in her seat and glanced back at the bathroom. "I'll be right back."

She burst through the lady's room door, the smell of vomit mixed with pine sol stung her nostrils. Jasmine was in a stall on her knees in front of the toilet bowl as Tina held her hair away from the puke.

"Doc is here," Sinclair said.

Jasmine heaved. "Oh no, tell him I'm sick. Tell him I can't make it, Sin."

Sinclair turned on her heels and marched out of the bathroom, bumping into Doc, who was standing outside the door.

He weaved from side to side, looking around Sinclair into the bathroom. "Jasmine. You okay in there?"

"Oh, no!" Jasmine said.

Alarmed, Doc side-stepped Sinclair into the lady's room and rushed toward Jasmine. He wet a paper towel and wiped her face with it, and took over the hair holding from Tina. "I got you," he said.

Tina and Sinclair looked at each other, not knowing how to take what they were seeing. Tina thought of the Huxtables and wondered if Jasmine even knew what she had in Doc. He was gentle, caring, and understanding of her illness and seemed to be exactly what she needed, at least at that moment anyway.

Doc stood Jasmine on her feet. "I'll see that she gets home safe," he said as he led her out of the bathroom.

They didn't doubt that he would.

CHAPTER 15

Tina pulled her car to the curb, shut off her engine and snapped on the steering wheel lock. She took a deep breath in through her nose and out through her mouth, waiting for the tightness in her chest to subside. A feeling she always got whenever she went back to the Cabrini Green projects she grew up in as a kid. She grabbed the grocery bags and finally stepped out of her car, walked past the kids playing stickball with a balled-up sock, just like she'd done at their age, past the broken entry door and into the foyer. The putrid smell of rotten garbage invaded her nostrils, and she pursed her lips, trying to avoid inhaling. She was surprised to discover the elevator wasn't broken and relieved when she made it to the eighth floor without it breaking down.

She stepped into a dark hallway as a necked bulb flickered overhead. Shifting the bag to her other hip she held the mace on her keychain with the other. Her father had given it to her when the crack epidemic ran rampant and crackheads roamed the hallways jacking folks for whatever they could steal. She reached the door where she had lived the better part of her life and knocked.

"Who is it?" a man's voice boomed from inside.

"It's me."

The door swung open. Like Tina, Odell Clemmons was short with an unruly salt and pepper afro and a full grey beard in need of a trim. His collared shirt was neatly pressed, and the creases in his pants were razor sharp. He smiled at Tina. "Where your key?"

"I didn't want to scare you," she said, stepping into the unit and placing the bags on the table.

It was a small two-bedroom unit. Tina had a room to herself growing up and her brothers shared the other. Her mother and father slept on a sofa bed in the living room before her mother left and never came back. The projects were supposed to be temporary living condition for the young family. Her father was a construction worker and her mother worked domestic but was going to secretary school and dreamed of getting a job in one of the office buildings along the Magnificent Mile. After her mother up and left the family one day out of the blue, her father struggled, not only financially but became an emotionally bankrupt, functional alcoholic. She never saw him sloppy drunk like Jasmine had gotten the other night. He was a quiet drunk. He'd work all week without a drop of alcohol, then come home Fridays after work with a case of beer, drowning his sorrows into the last can, before getting up bright and early Monday morning to do it all over again.

"Can't scare me. I knew you were coming." He walked slightly bent over, shoveling one foot in front of the other. He'd been injured on the job a few years back and was on disability now, unable to work. The one thing he had done right was get into the union, so he had a pension to lean on, just enough to maintain his dismal existence.

"You eat something today?" Tina asked, putting the bag of groceries away.

He'd shuffled back to the couch, where he still slept, even though he now lived in the unit alone. Tina had gotten free cable working at Kahn and he'd become obsessed with the hundreds of basic cable channels now at his disposal. He didn't know Tina knew that he'd also added the premium Playboy channel to his account. He'd tried dating after her mother left. Tina remembered a few women who tried to take her mother's place, but between three rambunctious boys, the drinking, and Tina's rebelliousness, no one ever stayed for long. It saddened Tina to know that she and her siblings played a part in her father's now lonely existence.

Tina placed a chicken on the counter and the ingredients she needed to prepare a meal for her father. She sat at the table and pulled out the prescriptions she'd picked up for her father and read the label of the new drug the doctor had prescribed. Odell was yelling at the television telling the game show contestants to select curtain number three when Tina heard a voice behind her.

"What you yelling about in here?" He stood in the doorway of her brother's old room in sweats and a t-shirt. Tattoos covered his chest and bulging arms from years of prison workouts.

Tina looked at the man like she saw a ghost. She looked at her father, who avoided her eyes, then back at the man in the doorway. "When did you get out? Daddy, you didn't tell me Stanley was out."

"Hey, sis!" He walked over to Tina, his arms stretched out, "I ain't been here but a few days. Pops told me you'd be here today, so we figured we'd surprise you."

Tina was in shock. Her brother Stan went to prison when she was in high school. He had been locked up for over ten years, and it had been a few years since she'd gone to visit. She'd fallen on hard times of her own and just didn't have the energy to make the trek to the state penitentiary in Joliet to visit, even though it was less than an hour away.

"Get up and give me a hug, girl."

Tina rose to her feet. She was trying to block out the pain she felt from losing her brothers to the penal system. Even though they were all older, she'd felt guilty when she couldn't keep the family together after her mother left. She was the only girl, and if her mother wasn't there to take care of the family, she'd conjured up in her ten-year-old mind that it was up to her. Stanley was the oldest, and while he looked after her when they were growing up, she felt it her ultimate responsibility to do for her brothers what their absent mother wasn't around to do, just like the mothers on the old television re-runs she watched as a kid. Stanley wrapped his arms around his sister as she melted into his strong embrace, but she couldn't help but wonder, now what? What would this uneducated, unskilled, black male ex-convict do with his life in the streets of Chicago living in the Cabrini Green housing project, and what type of strain would it put on her father?

Stan held her at arms-length, studying every inch of her. "You look good, little sis!"

She smiled at her brother as the tightness in her chest returned. "What's your next move?" she said, placing the prescription bottle down on the table. She moved to the counter and began cutting up the chicken.

Stan sat at the table. "Well, since I been rehabilitated, the sky's the limit, right?" he said, picking up the pill bottle and reading the label.

Tina watched Stan study the labels on all Odell's prescriptions as she seasoned and floured the chicken. She put a pot of water on the stove to boil and spooned Crisco into a pan to let it get hot while she cut up potatoes and snapped green beans. She took a deep breath in through the nose and out through the mouth, trying to convince herself that Stanley being home was a good thing. He would be there to take care of daddy, and she wouldn't have to worry about him so much, but that didn't relieve the tightness in her chest, so she just kept taking deep breaths.

"Pop tells me you got into college?" Stan said, his question more a surprise than an inquiry.

"That's right," she said, dropping the potatoes into the boiling water. I start in the fall.

They chatted more about what she'd been up to. About her work at Kahn and how she was homeless before Odell hooked her up with his old friend, Lincoln, who was the install supervisor there. She told him that Andrew, the youngest of the brothers, had called from prison, and she'd sent him money. Andrew had been sent to Danville, a new correctional facility in Illinois that housed medium-security prisoners, unlike Stan, who had done hard time in the old state prison in Joliet.

Stan reminisced about how he had arrived there shortly after the cell block take-over by the Black P. Stone Nation street gang. The word on the street was that they ran the prison. While Stan hadn't been a part of the gang, he knew some of the members from around the Green and got the notion in his young, dumb brain that pulling time would be a cake walk. Even though Odell did the best he could to ensure his boys had everything they needed to survive the hard streets they lived in, his job and drinking prevented him from giving them what they needed the most—his time. So, when Stan robbed that convenience store with those other boys, it got him a ticket to Joliet and the hard-core reality that his time was not going to be the walk in the park he envisioned.

"Man, if I knew then what I know now," he said. "Lot of cats didn't make it out of that place alive. I gotta give it up for Pops. He taught us if they don't involve you, don't get involved. I kept my head down and my mouth shut." He looked over at his dad, who was watching another game show. "Ain't that right, Pops?"

Odell was fixated on the television. "Hot dog, she done won that car. You see this, Tina?" he said, his excitement as if he'd won himself.

"Yeah, daddy. Go on and get washed up. Food's ready. You too, Stan. We still wash our hands before we eat in this house."

Stan rubbed his hands together. "And it's smelling good too, don't have to ask me twice. Come on, Pops." He went to the couch to help Odell up.

"I can get up," Odell said, swatting him away. Stan stood by and watched his dad make his way slowly to the bathroom before following behind him.

Tina fixed the plates for her father and brother like she did when they all crowded into the apartment together for dinner time back in the day. She took the cold pitcher of water from the fridge, poured a pack of Kool-Aid and a cup of sugar and stirred it until it dissolved. Placing the plates on the table, she stopped in her tracks—one of her father's medicine bottles was missing. She breathed deeply through her nose and out through her mouth.

Stan came out of the bathroom, "This gon' be a treat, sis. I ain't had a home-cooked meal in over ten years."

Tina stood by the table, one hand on her hips and the other out, palm up. Stan looked at his sister. She wasn't the pubescent teenager he'd left behind over ten years ago.

"I was just making sure Pop didn't overdo it with them pills. That Vicodin what them movie stars be OD'ing on." He took the bottle of pills out of his pocket and placed them in Tina's palm. "I read all about that shit when I was locked up."

"Well, you not locked up no more, Stanley. So, bury that prison mentality. You with family now. We don't steal from each other."

"I wasn't stealing. Ah, man!! How I'm stealing and you standing right here? I know you knew it was there. Come on, sis. Give me some credit.'

She pointed toward the bathroom door. "He ain't the same man you left behind all them years ago. That accident left him broken in more ways than one, and you can't come back here making things worse than they already are. You gotta be part of the solution, Stanley, 'cause we got all the problems we need!" Tina held back the tears that were stinging her eyes.

"You got me all wrong," Stan persisted. "I'm just—"

"What's all that ruckus out here?" Odell shuffled from the bathroom to the kitchen table.

"Nothing, Daddy. Come on, eat your food." She shook a pill out of each of the other prescription bottles. "The doctor changed your prescription."

"Good. Cause them other ones give me gas," Odell said, taking his seat at the table.

She put the pills in his hand and handed him a glass of Kool-Aid. "You gotta take them with food, one every day, ok?

"Just put 'em in that pillbox I keep over there; it'll help me remember. Ain't nothing wrong with my mind. Body just a little broken up is all."

"You been in any pain," she asked him.

"Naw. I'm good. I don't want take them pills he give me for pain, make me sleepy can't watch my shows. You get my liniment?"

"Yeah, I got it."

"That's all I need. Rub some of that on the pain, I'm good," Odell said, taking a bite of his drumstick.

"Ok, if you need the pills, just let me know," she said, putting the bottle of Vicodin in her pocket. She glanced over at Stan. "I'll bring you some."

Odell took a fork full of mashed potatoes and snap beans. "You put your foot in this, girl." He watched his son shove food in his mouth like he had a time limit to finish. "Slow down, son. There's more where that came from. You home now."

Tina finally sat down to eat, she took a deep breath in through her nose and out through her mouth.

CHAPTER 16

Charmaine laid awake in her bunk bed, staring at the water-stained ceiling in the group home she shared with seven other girls and the group home counselor. It was Saturday, and they were allowed to sleep in until nine-thirty, a reframe from the early morning weekdays when their bus arrived at seven a.m. to take them to multiple schools. The girls in the group home ranged from age twelve to seventeen, and they all attended different schools throughout the Chicago school system. She didn't think about them often, but this morning her parents were on her mind. She wasn't sure if Jasmine's drunken insults reminded her of her father or that this was the first time she had been away from them so long. The group home counselor, Sherri, had helped her register with the Cook County Jail for visits, but she hadn't been able to bring herself to go. She lay there, thinking about how a seemingly normal middle-class household like hers could land her in a place like this. Most of the girls in the home had a long history of abandonment and abuse and had been shuffled from one foster home to the next. The group home was where they were placed by the state when they were between foster care. At their ages, most stayed in group homes until they aged out because most families didn't want teenagers.

She closed her eyes and envisioned happier times when she'd run in the sand at the 67th Street Beach while her parents lounged nearby on a blanket. They'd enjoy a picnic lunch, and when their food was digested, her father would take her out in the water for a swim lesson. She let the feeling of those days rush over her, pushing out the memories of how the crack epidemic grabbed her parents by the neck and chocked any signs of common sense out of them. It started slowly, their neighbor bringing the powder drug with him to their lively competitive bid whist games on the weekend. She remembered her mother fusing at her dad when she walked in and saw him snort the cocaine up his nose while she was in the room. One day a funny smell wafted through the house, and she followed the scent to the kitchen where the bid whist game was played. Instead of slinging cards across the table, they passed around a pipe, the competition now over who got to hit it next; the deck of cards lay unshuffled on the table.

The more her father abused that pipe, the more he became verbally abusive towards Charmaine and her physical appearance. She buried her head in the pillow, trying to block out the words and images of her father. He'd call her a nasty lesbian when she was twelve years old, and she had to look it up in the dictionary to find out what it meant. She remembered how reading the meaning of that word made her cry. She wasn't sure if it was because of what was happening inside of her when she looked at girls who had already begun to sprout breasts, making her wonder what they looked and felt like, or that she preferred pants and sneakers over dresses. Did that make her this word that she was reading about? She also liked how a boy in class smelled like Ivory soap and made her heart flutter when he smiled at her. Did Lesbians like boys who smiled?

She was now sixteen and had been made so confused by the names her father called her. She didn't hate men, just hated that her father, the first man in her life, treated her so mean. She didn't know what she liked. Unlike Jasmine's tortured remark, she didn't know if she wanted dick or pussy. What she did know was that it was her damn business and her damn choice.

She checked the clock. It was still quiet in the room, and everybody was still sleeping or pretending they were. She figured she'd be the first in the bathroom. There were assigned chores that had to be completed before being allowed to leave the group home for the day, and she wanted to get an early start before heading to the fourplex. She was excited about trying out some of the decorating tips she'd picked up at the seminar. If there were such things as angels, she'd decided that Sinclair was hers. She never knew she loved decorating or was so good at it until she met Sinclair, who was also teaching her what acceptance looked and felt like, and she welcomed that in her life of judgment. The examples of going after whatever you wanted were life's gold nuggets that she owed all to Sinclair. She felt a sense of belonging by being a part of making the fourplex look fabulous or, as Sinclair would say, profitable.

She hopped off the bunk and tiptoed across the room to her dresser drawer to get what she needed for the bathroom. She was an only child and had a hard time adjusting to the shared room, drawers and bathroom space. Moving quietly out the door and down the hall, she ran into Sherri, the group home counselor.

"You're up early?" Sherri beamed.

Charmaine liked Sherri. If anyone had found their calling, Sherri had. She was a natural caregiver with positive words for everyone she met. She was always encouraging the girls to live up to their potential. There were positive posters throughout the home with quotes from everyone, from Zora Neal Hurston to Maya Angelou.

"Getting an early start on the bathroom?" Charmaine said. "Got a busy day. Heading over to Sinclair's after chores."

A concerned look washed over Sherri's face.

"Don't worry," Charmaine said, "I'll make curfew. I always do."

"Always, but—" Sherri didn't get to finish. Charmaine had already closed the door to the bathroom.

She stripped down and turned the water on in the shower, and just before she stepped in, she caught her reflection in the mirror. At sixteen, she still hadn't fully developed. She lacked the breast that caught her curiosity when her friends developed them at twelve and thirteen, and her hips and waist were void of any curves. She was a straight line from her armpit to her toes. She wore her clothes baggy because she was so skinny, she thought it made her look heavier. She couldn't envision that years from now people would envy her metabolism. Her hair touched her shoulders but lacked any style, so she wore it pulled back in a ponytail all the time. This is who she was, she thought and was perplexed by why it made people so crazy.

Once dressed, she started on her chores, which for the week were sweeping inside and out and watering the plants and garden. Sherri had engaged them all in a raised bed garden project, and Charmaine actually enjoyed seeing the fruits of her labor turn into actual edible products. She picked some tomatoes and peppers and carried them inside to the kitchen.

"Look at these bad boys," Charmaine said to Sherri, who was making breakfast. She searched the cabinets for the colander. "They gon' make a great omelet or salad later."

She hadn't noticed the woman in the green suit sitting at the table or the look on Sherri's face.

"Charmaine, I want to introduce you to Miss Grey."

Charmaine turned, noticing the woman for the first time. "Hi. I'm Charmaine,"

"Pleased to meet you," Miss Grey said.

Sherri and Miss Grey exchanged looks. Sherri let out a deep sigh. "Miss Grey is from the Department of Child and Family Services."

Charmaine looked up from her freshly picked vegetable. Whenever someone from the DCFS visited, it meant that someone was getting placed in foster care. From the horror stories she'd heard from the girls who'd been shuffled in and out of them, she was glad she had reached the expiration date by her age.

"Oh, oh. Who this time?" Charmaine said, already feeling sorry for the housemate that got assigned.

Sherri couldn't find the words, but Miss Grey had no problem. "We've found a nice family for you."

Charmaine twisted her head toward Miss Grey and glared into her face trying to comprehend the words that had come out of her mouth. "For who?"

"They're a couple out in Deerfield—"

"Deerfield!!" Charmaine looked over at Sherri. "What I do? I always made curfew. Why you doing this?"

Agonized, Sherri tried to explain, "I don't have a say. I told them you were thriving here."

Charmaine turned to the intruder in the suit, "See, thriving. Tell them thank you, but no thank you."

"I'm sorry. It doesn't work like that. Your parents have been sentenced, and the courts think it's best you be placed on permanent housing," Miss Grey said.

"Sentenced. I didn't know they'd been—"

"You haven't bothered to go see them. Ms. Sherri tells me she helped you with the visiting—"

"Is that why I'm being punished, cause I didn't go see my parents?" Charmaine said.

Sherri took her hand, "No, sweetie, we're not punishing you at all. The state just feels—"

"But how?" Charmaine was crying now, "How can they know. There ain't no black people in Deerfield."

"There's a growing black community there. Well, this couple is mixed," Miss Grey assured her. "The mother's black, but she and her husband both feel it would be nice for their young daughter to have a big sister."

"A black sister, you mean. Out there with all them white folks, she's probably getting her ass kicked every day. Well, I ain't her goddamn bodyguard!" Charmaine yelled.

"Calm down. It's not like that," Miss Grey turned to Sherri. "You were supposed to have her prepared for this."

"I thought the director had told her. I didn't get the news until this morning; it wasn't until I saw her that I realized she hadn't been told."

"I'm sorry. But you'll have to pack and come with me. Next week is spring break and you'll start school out there after that. It's all been worked out. It'll be good for you."

"I'm a junior in high school. I already got my classes planned for next semester, and I got new friends here. How can this be good for me? HOW CAN THIS BE GOOD FOR ME?!!"

CHAPTER 17

 By the calendar, spring had sprung but forgot to let Chicago know. I grabbed my mink coat, a gift to myself, and headed out into the cold night, thankful that Tina had negotiated that new battery in my car. It turned right over, and I headed north toward the Magnificent Mile. I was dressed to impress in a black two-piece suit with a fuchsia-colored camisole. It was a business reception hosted by real estate developers, and while I wanted to look professional, Grandmama Pearl had taught me that a little bit of sexy never hurt.

Kash had invited me and even told me to bring the kid, referring to Charmaine. "Charmaine has a curfew." I told him without revealing too much about her business. Besides, I hadn't told him that she'd gone AWOL on me. I knew she was probably still hurt by Jasmine's nonsense and had every right to be. I figured I'd give her a little space. She'd come around eventually. I hadn't even talked to Jasmine since that night. I was used to her getting drunk and saying crazy things about people, but what she did to Charmaine was downright mean, and when I was ready to deal with her, I intended to tell her so.

Deja vu swept through me as I pulled the car into the circular drive of the Drake Hotel and the white-gloved attendant escorted me out of my car. I entered the hotel and made my way to the elevator and up to the reception area. It wasn't the penthouse ball-room as it had been the night Trace and I was there a few years ago, but the venue was just as grand. The setting was more intimate in a small reception hall on the mezzanine overlooking the Gold Coast. I was met by waiters passing trays of champagne and hors d'oeuvres.

This was not a mixed crowd like the one I attended with Trace. Here, a few other black folks and I stuck out like a sore thumb among the white republican elite of Chicago. I summoned Trace's spirit and waltzed into the room like I already had McCormick money. The heads turned and I put on my approachable mug—the cheese-eating grin that black folks have had to perfect to disarm such a crowd as this. I nodded hello to a few friendly faces, and as I made my way across the room, I saw Kash out of the corner of my eye, heading my way.

"Nice threads," Kash said, rubbing the back of his hand along the mink.

"Fake it till you make it," I said.

"You fit right in with that. Don't let these honkey's fool you; most of them trying to get it, just like us. I'ma introduce you to the movers and the shakers. The ones got them deep pockets. Them the ones you want to know when it come time to get some of that—"

"McCormick money," we said in unison, laughing at ourselves.

Kash lifted a glass of champagne from a tray and guided me to a bar table. I took in the crowd as he pointed out certain people, from the presidents of banks to developers of some of the major projects in Chicago, to politicians.

Kash pointed to a black man across the room. "Over there is Melvin Tanner, he's—"

"That Alderman people been gossiping about."

"The way I hear it, that gossip about to get real. Old boy stuck his hands in the wrong cookie jar."

"Yeah, I hear he forgot to share," I said, watching Tanner as he worked the room, his short-pudgy frame gliding through the crowd, shaking hands. His staffer nearby feeding him the names of the folks clamoring to get a few minutes with him.

Kash looked around the room. "To your left, with the red tie, that's the cat they tagging to take his seat."

I looked at the man Kash had pointed out. He was young, tall, handsome and white. "Him? Tanner's ward is all black. That won't go over well."

"That's who they pushing." Kash said, taking shrimps on a stick from a waiter and handing me one.

"Who is they?" I asked, taking a nibble of shrimp.

"Girl, keep up," Kash said, with a mouth full of shrimp. "All these developers up in here, that's who they is. Why you think they're throwing this shindig."

"Mayor Washington has control of the council now," I said as a proud supporter who worked on his campaign and the council war he gained a victory over last year.

"He just one vote. Twenty-five Alderman gotta vote his way, and his boy Tanner won't count." He gestured to the room. "Look around you, they in here soliciting votes for their guy right now.

Kash pointed out people around the room. I'd worked on Mayor Washington's campaign and became familiar with the fifty-member city council. I recognized a few of the Aldermen, some of who were Washington supporters, hobnobbing with the developers and contractors that were out to place a Washington opposition on the council. Kash was right, if Tanner got indicted and subsequently suspended from his seat, that could change the entire dynamics of the council—giving favor to the developers to the detriment of the low-income constituents of that predominantly black ward.

"So, by the time the motion gets to chambers—"

"It's a done deal. Them votes being determined tonight."

I dismissed the whole thing. "If it even happens. There's always rumors about corrupt Chicago politicians."

"And always convictions, cause they all repeat the same dumb moves. Chicago politicians keep the Feds in business."

I was about to respond but held my comment as a man and woman approached the table. I immediately spotted the rock on her finger and the diamonds dangling from her ears. Her companion sported a Gucci suit and wore a Rolex. He patted Kash on the back like they were old friends.

"Kingsley, nice to see you. You met my wife."

"Good evening, Bob. Pleasure seeing you again, Candy, right?

"That's right."

A fitting name for a woman dripping in jewels, I thought.

Let me introduce you to a colleague of mine," Kash said, gesturing toward me. "Sinclair Ellis meet Bob and Candy Albright

I held in my laugh, smiling instead at Candy and Bob. "Nice meeting you," I said, trying not to burst out at Kash's altered dialect; his entire voice had changed.

"Bob's the President of Albright Savings and Loan," Kash said.

My insides settled when I heard that. I remembered Kash and my conversation at the real estate seminar. He was playing his white side for the McCormick money he had his eye on. I didn't have that luxury, so I used my years of maneuvering in the white world as my guide. People liked to talk about themselves, so I gave Bob and Candy the floor.

"I bet that keeps you busy. What do you do when you're not analyzing spreadsheets?" I asked.

Candy answered for him. She linked her arm through his and snuggled close to him. "Bob's an excellent painter," she said. "His work has been featured in a few galleries in Chicago."

Smiling, Bob patted her arm. "She announces that every chance she gets," Bob said.

"As she should," I said, connecting with Candy. "What galleries? I'd love to see your work."

I kept them talking about themselves for the next ten minutes. Kash and I gave each other non-verbal cues on controlling the conversation, and he jumped in on cue to bring it back to real estate.

"We have several of his pieces at our condo on Lakeshore," Candy said. "Our decorator has done a marvelous job displaying them."

"Sinclair is working with a decorator on a fourplex she's rehabbing in Hyde Park."

"Oh, I just love Hyde Park." Candy said, singing the words. It's such a nice historical community. It's going to be the place to be in a few years. Just mark my words."

A place for who, I thought, because we're already there.

"What's your plans for the property?" Bob asked.

"Fix and flip," I said as the waiter passed by and we all grabbed a fresh glass of champagne.

Bob pulled out his card and handed it to me. "Give me a call when you're ready for your next one. We've got some great programs for investors, especially for improvement projects in the urban area," he said with ease.

Candy took his card and pulled a Monte Blanc from her purse, "Here's my number. Let me know when you want to check out the galleries. I'll give you a personal tour of Bob's work."

I took the card, turning it from front to back, "I will and I will," I said to them both.

Kash made the next move. "I see someone over there I want to introduce you to, Sinclair. Bob, Candy, pleasure seeing you again," he said, shaking hands,

"All mine," Bob said. He tipped his champagne glass toward me, "And I look forward to hearing from you, young lady."

Kash led me away. "Ok, you better work it! I'ma take lessons from you."

"Look who's talking with your 'Hi Bob, How are you. What a pleasure'," I said, mocking him.

Kash laughed, "Hey, when in Rome," he said. "We got to use what we got to get what we want."

We clinked our champagne glasses together. "Touché," I said, giggling, enjoying the moment when a familiar voice floated above the chatter, and I turned to see Carla talking to a group behind me. I swiveled back around, wearing my discomfort on my sleeve.

Concerned, Kash looked in the direction of my discomfort. "Who that?"

"Nobody," I said, walking away from the area.

"Wait, want to introduce you to the cat she's talking to."

I kept walking toward the buffet table. As the night went on, they'd stopped passing hors d'oeuvres and had a full spread in the back of the room. "Maybe later. What is she even doing here?" I said mostly to myself.

"Whoever she is, she's got you spooked," Kash said, handing me a small plate. "That Alderman she's talking to is on the City Zoning Committee; we certainly want him on our side."

"I don't have a side. What are you talking about?"

"Ah man, girl, you killing me," he said exasperated. "The developer's side. Our side. You a developer now. We need folks in high places to make them McCormick deals."

We walked through the buffet line, piling food on our plates. I hadn't mentioned to Kash that I had called off my wedding. Didn't engage him about my ex-fiancé, who some people were also tapping for that empty Alderman seat if Tanner was indicted. I surely wanted to avoid explaining that his mother, his biggest cheerleader, was chumming up with council members to sway the vote their way. Nope, wasn't having that conversation tonight.

I got to the end of the buffet line, turned to look for a seat to chow down, and smashed right into Carla—butter-crusted baked salmon, roast beef and horseradish sauce, salad with olive oil dressing—ran down her blouse.

"Oh my god," I said. "What… Why are you standing behind me like that?"

She snatched the napkin from my hand and started brushing the food from her silk blouse. "I saw you and was coming to say hello."

She was coming to gloat. To rub my face in the fact that I wasn't marrying her son. "Hello," I said, ditching the spilled plate on a passing waiter's tray.

"I haven't seen you since you called off the wedding. How are you?"

"Great. I have a lot going on. Bye, Carla," I said, walking away.

"Danny's not doing so great," she shouted behind me.

Carla had a knack for sticking her nose where it didn't belong. I felt relief knowing that her meddling wasn't going to govern my life. Whatever Danny was going through was his business. I pivoted and tried to cut her with my cold stare. There was a lot I wanted to say, to shout at her and tell her, "It's your fault. He's not doing great because of you! We were doing just fine before you stuck your nose in our business. You're a controlling, meddling, hoovering bitch of a mother, and you're running his life!" But it wasn't worth it, so I just lied and said, "I'm sorry about your blouse," and marched out of the room.

Kash fell in step next to me. "Damn, baby girl, you didn't tell me you escaped the ball and chain. Whoever he was, he wasn't ready for you. I see right now, you need a real man. Weak joker won't be down with what you trying to do. Too intimidating. They'll just hold you back," he said, opening the door for me as we strolled out into the valet area.

We handed the valet our tickets as I took a deep breath, trying to steady my trembling hands. Kash fell silent. He seemed to intuitively know when to talk and when not. He walked me to the car. As the valet opened the door, I handed him a tip and got in.

Kash leaned in, "Nice ride," he said. He grabbed my hands to steady them before looking me in the face. "McCormick money. That's what you are, and that back there," he said, squeezing my hands a little tighter, "Is just a minor inconvenience, don't let it shake you."

CHAPTER 18

"I don't remember any of that," Jasmine said. "How is she?"

"She hasn't come around since," Sinclair said, stopping for a moment to kick the sand out of her flip flops.

Like the politics in Chicago, the weather had abruptly changed from mink coat weather to flip flops over a few days. The whole city seemed to migrate outdoors for some fun in the sun activity, knowing that it could change again in a matter of hours.

A frisbee floated their way, and Tina tried throwing it back to the group of kids playing in the sand, but the wind caught it, sailing it through the air and landing it near the water's edge. "I tried, she said, shrugging at the boy that ran to get it. "What *do* you remember, Jas?"

Jasmine had been trying to do just that since the morning she woke up and found Doc sleeping on her couch. He jumped up when she came in from the bedroom, holding her pounding head. She was no stranger to hangovers, but this one had her cross-eyed.

"I got just what you need," Doc said. He sat her down, went into the kitchen and brought back a glass of water and some toast. "Sip this," he said, handing her the water. I tried to get some in you last night before you went to bed."

It was then that Jasmine noticed she was in her pajamas. "She leaped up from her seat, but her pounding head forced her back down on the couch. Moaning, she buried her head in the pillow, "What happened? Where are my clothes? What are you even doing here?"

"We had a date last night, remember?" he said, handing her half of the toast.

Jasmine turned her head like a toddler, "No, I don't want it," she said, pushing the toast away.

"You need something in your stomach. I'm telling you, you'll feel better. Trust me."

Jasmine walked alongside Tina and Sinclair. The Chicago Skyline peeked out around the bend. "I remember waking up and Doc was on my couch," Jasmine said. "He told me that he came to pick me up and I was sick in the bathroom. Didn't really get into it much."

She didn't want to tell them what Doc told her about his own journey. She remembered taking the piece of toast and watching him watch her chew it.

"You been here all night?" she asked him.

He nodded. "I put the towels I used to clean up in the hamper. You may want to laundry them soon, so they don't smell up the place."

"Clean up what?" Jasmine asked, washing down the toast with the water.

Hesitant, Doc cocked his head to the side, "Ah, well, you threw up a little bit. Well, a lot."

Jasmine buried her face in her hands, "Oh my god, how embarrassing." It must have been something I ate. I don' get sick from... sorry... damn, thank you."

"Nothing to be sorry about. I've been there. AA and the whole nine yards."

"But you drink; you've brought wine," she said.

"It was a long time ago. I was a teenager. I'm wiser now; know my limit. It's all about moderation," he said, getting up to fill her glass with more water.

The ladies came to a stop near rocks that jetted out over Lake Michigan and sat down to enjoy the breeze coming around the bend. It was still a little chilly, but this felt balmy after the freezing temperatures they'd been experiencing. They all sat there for a minute in their own thoughts.

Sinclair's mind drifted to the first time she and Trace made love on the rocks overlooking Lake Michigan. She thought about what Kash said about her needing a real man. Trace wouldn't have been intimidated by what she was doing. He'd be her biggest cheerleader, maybe not the most committed one, but an encouragement just the same.

Tina worried about her dad and if Stanley being home with him would be a blessing or a curse. She'd been trying to think of a way to help him get on his feet so that he didn't slip back into breaking the law to survive. She wanted to ask *him* to give her brother a job but had to wait until the next time they got together. She could explain Stan's situation, helping him avoid having to check the box—*have you ever been arrested or convicted of a crime*—the endless prosecution that landed convicts right back in jail.

Jasmine racked her brain, trying to remember what happened at the restaurant. It was pretty much a blank after the waitress brought the meals to the table. The next thing she remembered was waking up and finding Doc on her couch.

"I need to apologize to Charmaine," Jasmine finally said

Sinclair chunked a rock into the lake. "You think?!" If she ever comes back over."

"I don't blame her," Tina said. She gave Jasmine the side-eye.

"If someone told me I didn't like dick. Talking all under my clothes, I'd ghost them, too."

Indignant, Jasmine put her hands on her hips, "Naw, I didn't say that."

"Girl, please. You were a hot mess," Tina said.

Jasmine dropped her head. "She hasn't called you, Sin?"

Sinclair sighed. "I got a new number when I moved to the four-plex, and I just never gave it to her. I pretty much knew her schedule, and she could stop by anytime."

"I'm so sorry. Do you know where she lives?"

"Yeah, I took her home once."

Jasmine stood up. "Then let's go."

Tina and Sinclair looked up at her.

"Get up. I've got to make this right."

Tina stood up. "You can start by not drinking so much," Tina said, shaking her head from side to side to the beat of each syllable.

Jasmine sucked her teeth, "Girl, I'm fine. It was something I ate. Food poisoning, or something."

"No, I'm pretty sure it was something you drank," Sinclair said, stepping down off the rocks.

They made it back to the car and headed toward the group home. Sinclair popped in a cassette she had made, and they jammed to commercial-free music. Singing out loud, snapping their fingers, and bobbing their head to her playlist. By the time they pulled up in front of the group home, they were high on Michael Jackson's *Man In The Mirror*. Tina leaned in from the back seat and sang loud in Jasmine's ear. "…*and I'm asking him to change his ways…*'

Jasmine swatted at Tina, like a fly was buzzing in her ear. She looked up at the well-kept house Sinclair had parked in front of. "Do we just walk up and knock on the door?"

"I don't see why not. It's a group home, not prison." Sinclair said.

They got out of the car and stood looking up at the house. It was a bungalow on a quiet street in Calumet Heights. They started up the walkway when a middle-aged woman came out onto the porch and greeted them from the top of the stairs. "Good afternoon, young ladies. How can I help you?"

Sinclair stepped forward. "Hi, I'm Sinclair. We're friends of Charmaine. She around?"

The women walked down the steps toward them. "Oh yes, she talked about you. The real estate lady, right? I'm Sherri. Nice to meet you."

"Kind of. She's been helping me with my rehab."

"She was so excited about that rehab. She really liked you?"

They looked around, confused. "Was?" Tina asked

"What happened to her? Is she alright?" Sinclair asked, quickening her pace down the walkway.

Sherri met them at the bottom of the stairs. "She'll be fine. DCFS came. You know I... I don't have much say... They place the girls." She stopped talking and took a deep breath. "Charmaine really liked it here. She was thriving, but—"

"Where is she?" Jasmine asked?

Sherri wrung her hands, "Oh my. They took her last week. Placed her in a home in Deerfield."

"Deerfield!!" They all screamed at once.

Sinclair squeezed her head between her hands. "What the... whose bright idea was that?"

Disgusted, Tina stomped her feet. "Department of Child and Family Services," she said, remembering how social workers used to come around Cabrini Green, checking on welfare recipients, sometimes causing more harm than good.

Jasmine spoke up. "We can't leave her out there."

"You're doggone right we can't," Sinclair said.

"Oh good," Sherri said. "I've been sick about it ever since they took her. There was no way to reach you, and her parents... well, they're no help, are they?" She started walking toward the house. "Come with me. I'll give you all the information I have." She stopped and turned toward them, sticking her finger in the air, "but you didn't get it from me."

"Get what?" Sinclair said as she marched up the stairs.

CHAPTER 19

"**P**lease. *Please stop. You said you wouldn't no more. OUCH! OUCH! STOP IT!! AUNT MATTIE, HELP—*
SMACK! *A hand landing across the screaming mouth.*

The sting in my face snatched me from the nightmare. My pajamas were drenched with sweat and my heart pounded like a jackhammer. I swung the covers aside and sat on the side of the bed pressing hard against my chest to steady it.

"No, no, no," I whispered into the darkened room, breathing slowly in and out. "They can't be back. They can't."

My body moved slowly across the room toward the bathroom, turning the faucet on full blast. The cold water stung my face and brought an odd sense of relief at the same time. I cursed my reflection in the mirror for insisting that I no longer needed therapy. I'd started it after the attack by Yusef uncovered memories of my abuse by Uncle Ervin. It had been buried so deep in my subconscious, only surfacing in nightmares that haunted me for years.

After several months of therapy, the nightmares stopped and I concluded that I was cured. Dr. Bello insisted on continuing the sessions, but between wedding planning, leaving Kahn and searching for my first property, it was an unnecessary distraction, so I hadn't gone in over a year.

Standing in the kitchen window as the coffee maker sputtered the last drop of water, the sounds of the springtime finally making its annual debut, did little to calm my nerves. Getting an appointment with Dr. Bello was like moving a mountain, but I decided it would be the first task of the day. It was still early and the sun was just peeping through the trees. I sat at the table, trying to push down the awful memories that had invaded my sleep. Dr. Bello had warned that stress could bring about episodes of nightmares if regular therapy sessions were stopped. I didn't feel stressed; sure, there were things going on, but that's life. It's always something, as Aunt Mattie used to say.

The hot coffee brought some comfort to my weary state of mind. It wasn't a daily habit, but coffee soothed me during troubled times. It reminded me of early mornings when I'd get up and sit with Grandmama Pearl. She'd make a cup of coffee for her and one for me. It was years later before learning that mine was mostly milk, just like I drink it now. Grandmama Pearl's gentle caring filled in for my mother, who was unable to be a mother to me after her breakdown. The continuity of that love made a world of difference in my life. Perhaps that's why I was drawn to Charmaine. Having been that girl, the different one always bullied for my appearance, the one with the crazy mother. I had no more control over my appearance than I did over my mother's illness. Still, I did find comfort in that duplex with my extended family, at least until Uncle Ervin attacked my innocence. Dr. Bello had explained that the trauma was too much for my young mind to process, so I pushed it so far down into the crevasse of my brain only to reveal itself in the deepest, darkest part of my soul until Yusef brought it back into the light.

The sun had made its grand appearance and promised a beautiful spring day. When the clock struck nine o'clock, I called Dr. Bello's office and made my appointment. It must have been exactly what I needed since, due to a cancellation, my appointment was set for later that week.

The din of the drill reverberated through the fourplex, signifying the crews had started work in the units. After a hot shower and breakfast, I caught up with Carlos for our daily morning progress report.

Carlos beamed with pride as he showed me the handy work on the main line pipe. I'd hung out enough around Uncle Ervin and his properties to know there was always a shortcut. It wasn't like this fourplex was my forever home; to spend thousands of dollars replacing a main line was not an option. After pushing Luisa to find another way, it turned out that placing a clamp on the damaged area could rectify the problem for years to come, or at least until I could sell the place.

"Muy Bueno!" I said to Carlos in my limited Spanish.

Carlos nodded and clasped his hands together. "Si, muy bueno! I very happy, you happy, Senorita Sinclair."

He handed me a work hat before allowing me to walk the work area. He and Luisa had applied for certification, and he didn't want to take the chance that a surprise inspection would catch him noncompliant with OSHA rules. He'd gotten a hat especially for me. I'd squirmed the first time he asked me to wear it.

"Whose head this been on?" I'd ask him, noticing my name misspelled across the front in magic marker.

He got that deer in a headlamp look, so I pointed to the inside of the hat and made a face, "Sucio," I said, remembering my high school Spanish, for dirty.

"No, Senorita, es new."

I took his word for it. Carlos didn't strike me as a liar.

We made our way to the kitchen as Luisa walked in. Her presence was a breath of fresh air. Not having to conjure up my old Spanish lessons helped me relax, knowing that I was clearly understood.

They were finally on the last unit and Luisa wanted to talk about tile selection for the kitchen and bath. Charmaine had decorated each unit with a slightly different color scheme and was looking forward to applying what she'd learned at the seminar to the last unit, but never got the chance. I told Luisa to copy the unit across the hall. Paint colors, fabric, and tile just wasn't my thing, and I knew how to stay in my lane. Of course, the walk-through couldn't be complete without presenting me with a problem they'd discovered the day before.

"Now, don't get upset, Miss Ellis," Luisa said. "We already have a cost-effective solution."

The term cost-effective was a sign that she was about to introduce me to an expensive problem. I followed her down the hall. Luisa pulled the rope to the attic access and let down the ladder, and I followed her up. She climbed in and straddled the beams in her work boots as I stood on the ladder and stuck my yellow hat through the entrance. Before she said anything, I already saw it.

"What the heck," I said.'

"Rats. Chewed right through the cable." Her flashlight traced the length of the electrical wire, "and see over here, this goes to the circuit box. We'll have to rip it out and replace it. Then—"

"How much," I said, climbing down the ladder. I'd seen enough.

She followed me down. "You're in luck. One of my guys is a licensed electrician, so we don't have to hire a sub. I have some wire leftover from another job, and he'll just charge you for the labor."

The labor charges were reasonable, so we made the deal and

Luisa and I walked out into the foyer. "You're a great client, Miss Ellis, and I hope to work with you a long time. I get the feeling you have many more properties in your future."

"That's the plan, Luisa, and if we're going to be working together, you might as well call me Sinclair.

I heard my phone ring in my apartment and I excused myself, taking two steps at a time to answer it before the answering machine. "Hello," I said, snatching the receiver off the hook.

The information Sherri had shared didn't include information on Charmaine's foster parents, just the name of the caseworker who placed her. I put in a call to the social worker who had helped Danny place Trevor and Josh and helped me get Charmaine into the group home. She was returning my call and told me that some of her cases had been reassigned due to her heavy workload, and a Miss Grey was in charge of Charmaine's file now.

"Thank you for calling back," I said. Miss Grey placed Charmaine in a home in Deerfield and—"

"Deerfield?"

"Yes, and I was wondering if you could get me a phone number or address or give her—"

"Giving out that information is against our policy, but...," I heard her rustling papers. "Did you say Deerfield?"

"Yes."

"Can I get back to you, Miss Ellis? I just want to check on a few things. Give me a couple of days."

"Sure. Is everything okay" I asked.

"Of course, of course, I just want to check on a few things with Ms. Grey. I'll call you in a few days."

"Okay," I said, sitting down at the table and using the unpacked box in front of me as an ottoman.

Unpacked boxes cluttered my space since I moved in. The

breakup with Danny had hit me harder than I wanted to admit. Even after Jasmine and them rescued me from my pity party, the chore of canceling the caterer, venue, dress and other services weighed heavy on my heart. Tina got the bright idea to hold a wedding cancel party, and they all came over with wine and our favorite snacks. We each took a company to call and canceled the service, then wrote out two-hundred cancellation cards to mail to guests. When I did try to unpack, everything I touched reminded me of Danny. He'd spent a lot of time at my place, and it seemed everything I took out of a box reminded me of him, from his favorite coffee cup to his favorite lingerie. I did more crying than unpacking and eventually just gave up on it.

I lifted my foot from the box and started going through the contents. It was going to be a while before I was settled into a place to call my own. Life in the foreseeable future was going to be moving from one investment property to another, and it was time to purge. I started sorting items in piles of what I would keep, sell, and donate. The items that I was going to keep, I consolidated into boxes in preparation for my next move. Unlike my previous attempt at unpacking, I gained energy in the task. It signified an ending and a beginning and I was looking forward to what the future would bring.

By midafternoon I had sorted all the boxes and my growling stomach reminded me that I had skipped breakfast. I went to the kitchen and peered in the fridge when I heard someone shout my name, accompanied by a loud knock at the door.

I rushed to the door, "Who the—" I swung it open to face Tina, grinning in her Kahn Telecommunications work clothes. "Girl, you better—"

Tina laughed, "Thought I was the Po-Po?"

"What you doing here in the middle of the day," I said, shutting the door and walking back toward the kitchen.

Tina followed behind me, "Has some crews on this side of town. Checking to see if those clowns working or goofing off."

"Like you," I teased.

"Hey, I'm Field Supervisor now. Goofing off is built into my job description. Besides, girls got to eat. What you got to eat up in here?"

"Perfect timing. I was just about to fix something.?"

Tina looked around the apartment. "Well damn. Somebody found their second wind. Last time I was in here, it looked like a warehouse. What's in here?" she said, rustling through the boxes marked Goodwill.

"I gotta let go of some stuff. Crazy how one person can accumulate so much junk. I'm gonna be moving from pillar to post, I don't want to be lugging all that stuff with me."

"Hell, I can use some of this," Tina said, pulling Danny's favorite coffee mug out of the Goodwill box.

I hesitated for a minute, feeling some kind of way about it. Did I want to go to Tina's house and drink out of that mug? "I walked over and grabbed it out of her hand, "That has a crack in it," I lied. Here's a nice one." I handed her a different mug and threw the reminder of Danny in the trash. "Help yourself to anything in there," I said, taking bread, cheese and butter out of the fridge.

We chatted about everything. Kahn had grown since I left and Lincoln had promoted her and Moose to Field Supervisors. They both got company trucks they got to take home and had to make the installation schedule for their crews. They basically rode around all day checking on the installations in their area.

"If y'all doing all of that, what the heck is Lincoln doing?"

"Girl, you know Lincoln. He never did do much of nothing, if you ask me. Long as I make his ass look good, he stays out of my business and I stay out of his. Besides, when I'm finished with college, I'm moving on," Tina said, taking items she was claiming out of the boxes I had just neatly packed them in.

"Be sure to pack that stuff back up like I had it," I said, melting the butter in the pan.

She threw me a side-eye.

"I ain't playing. I spent all morning on that. Anyway, back to college," I said, doing a little dance. "I can't wait. You gonna kill it. I can tell that from that essay you wrote."

Tina cocked her head, "You mean the one you helped me write."

I laid the slices of bread in the butter and topped them with cheese. "It was your story; I just helped you rearrange the words a little."

The University began offering a program for adult learners who wanted to go to college. They streamlined the administration process and used life experience and letters of recommendation as the determining factor. Between Tina's junior college classes, that banging essay and recommendations from Kahn, she was accepted with flying colors.

"That was a whole lot of rearranging," she said, washing her hands and grabbing plates from the cabinet. "You know what I'm looking forward to the most?"

I slid the grilled cheese sandwiches onto the plates. "What's that?"

"My daddy seeing me walk across that stage and get my degree. I know he feels like a failure behind my jailbird brothers, but I want him to know that he did right by me."

"I'm sure he's proud of you either way. How are those brothers of yours," I said, grabbing a bag of chips and getting two cans of soda out of the fridge.

"Ugh, Stan is back."

That was another thing Tina and I bonded over. Having family members in jail wasn't anything rare where we came from. Most black families on the southside of Chicago, the west side of Gary, or any inner city in America did, it was all by design, but it still held a sort of stigma to it. My cousin Kyle and I were close as kids, and he was locked up again, and it was nice to connect with someone who knew what that felt like. Prison affected the whole family.

She took a bite of her grilled cheese sandwich, "Girl, please. I don't even want to talk about it. I'm just glad I can go back to my apartment and not have to deal with it twenty-four-seven. I am trying to see how I can help him not repeat. He was locked up a long time. I'ma ask a friend of mine if he…"

She didn't finish her sentence, just stopped and took a gulp of her soda.

I shrugged. "What friend?"

"Nobody you know," she said. "Thanks for the sandwich, girl. I better get back to work," she said, practically sprinting toward the door.

My instinct radar went off. My friend was hiding something, for sure.

CHAPTER 20

Asparrow sang just outside the open window and the breeze ushered in the scent of spring flowers in bloom. Mahogany and soapstone statues and bold, colorful fabrics and textures accented the chocolate leather furniture that felt like butter on my skin. In the corner, a small water fountain filled the room with a relaxing Zen that eased my anxiety about being there.

Across from the buttery leather couch where I sat, Dr. Bello crossed her legs and placed her notepad on her lap. She had a sweet face with high cheekbones and eyes that seemed to smile indefinitely. Her dashiki attire and afro hairstyle coordinated with the office décor adding to the serenity of a safe space.

My earlier visits here were mixed with a blend of sorrow, anger and guilt. Emotions I didn't even know I had about events in my life that surfaced and laid bare my innermost conflicts. I'd leave the sessions exhausted from the battles I had between facing the truth and continuing the lies that I'd hidden behind for so many years. Lies that masqueraded as my truth and propped me up with a false sense of security and confidence. The sessions with Dr. Bello taught me that I was more than my surface self. More than the face that I put to the world and had convinced myself was my total being.

To become whole again, I would have to peel back many layers of protection, like peeling away an old scab, opening up the sore and waiting on the healing to complete to allow the new skin to emerge. I'd convinced myself during the healing process that I was already healed and discontinued my sessions before the new skin could replace my pain. Just like an unhealed wound reopening from more trauma, the returning nightmares brought me back to begin the healing process all over again.

Not knowing what to expect from therapy sessions when first attending, I anticipated being asked many questions that I would ponder and respond to. Jasmine hadn't shared her therapy experience with me, and her therapist didn't think it ethical to treat us both for the same trauma from the same man, so she recommended I see Dr. Bello. After introducing herself during my first session, she asked me one question, "What positive changes would you like to see happen in your life?"

Stumped by this question, surely, she'd read the lengthy questionnaire she had me fill out before seeing me. It clearly spelled out my trauma, the attack by Yusef, and the childhood abuse by Uncle Ervin, neither of which had anything to do with how I lived my life, then or now. I didn't answer her, I laid silent, trying to figure out why she asked me that, repeating the question over and over again in my head.

I'd had many sessions with Dr. Bello since that day. Eventually, it became crystal clear why she had asked me that. She was leading with the end in mind. With the day when I could put all that trauma and abuse behind me and emerge in my new skin. I never answered that question that first day or during any session since, but I was prepared to answer it today.

"To not be lost," I said toward the end of our session. "To find myself, again."

Dr. Bello's eyes sparkled. She knew instinctively that I was referring to that question asked so many months ago. "And that change is within your reach." she said, "Simply let the healing process complete."

I was glad I had come. I made my next appointment with her secretary and since the appointment was on the near north side, it was a good time to reach out to Candy, Kash's connection from the real estate developer's reception we had attended.

We agreed to meet at the gallery where Bob's paintings were curated, then grab a quick bite for lunch. Cultivating that relationship was the smart thing to do. If I needed to, calling on Bob could fair in my favor if his wife and I were acquainted. It also showed that I was true to my word when I said I wanted to see his work. I arrived first and waited at a nearby bakery, purchased a Danish and orange juice, and sat in the window so that I could see Candy when she pulled up. The tap on my shoulder pulled my attention away from the window. I hadn't seen him since the day he walked out of my apartment.

"Danny," I said.

"Sinclair. How are you?"

We stood looking into each other's eyes, both so caught up in the awkward moment that I didn't notice the woman he was with, and he must have forgotten she was there until she cleared her throat, announcing her presence.

Danny didn't shift his gaze from mine. "I'll be out in a minute," he said, handing her the car keys.

Stunned, she rolled her eyes and left.

"A new attorney at the office," he said.

Danny's office wasn't far from Lincoln Park, but I figured the chances of running into him were one in a million.

"Look, Sinclair. I… I haven't…" he sighed and ran his hand over his head like he does when he's nervous. "I miss you, okay. Can we—"

A tapping on the window interrupted him. "Sinclair!" Candy

said in her sing, sing voice. "So, sorry I'm late," she said, making her way into the bakery. "I had a hair appointment this morning, and my, oh my, she took forever. I kept saying, Sally, I have somewhere I have to be, honey. Guess you can't rush beauty, huh?" She noticed Danny standing there. "Oh, my. He's handsome, just like the one the other night. Who are you?"

"Just an old friend," I answered, "He was just leaving. His colleague is waiting." I stood up. "I can't wait to see Bob's art." We walked out of the bakery and I put an extra sway in my hips as I felt Danny's eyes track me from the window.

In the session, I had assured Dr. Bello that I was over Danny and had moved on with my real estate deals. She was the only person I'd share my McCormick money dreams with. Kash came up in our discussion as well; like always, she did more listening than talking. Then asked me one of her open-ended questions, "What would it take for you to feel happier or more at peace?"

I knew better than to think her questions were out of the left field, but this I felt pretty sure about. "I'm at peace," I said.

Dr. Bello didn't respond; she wrote something down in her notebook and looked at me with that smiling face of hers.

Candy and I walked down the sidewalk to the gallery a few doors away. She talked incessantly, a trait that I hadn't noticed at the reception. She seemed more even keel; today, she was clearly tilting toward the left.

We stopped in front of a storefront with no sign out front. The façade was painted white except for the door, which was a deep purple. Candy rang the bell explaining that she'd made an appointment for a private viewing.

"You didn't have to go to that trouble for me," I said.

She waved it off. "No problem, Bob and I own a piece of the place. Young girl is nicely paid to open up for private viewings.

Makes it look legit," she said, as a stylishly dressed, chunky young brunette answered the door.

Behind the purple door of this nondescript building, paintings lined either side of the wall. A spiral staircase led to a loft that was decked out with a bar and seating area. Track lights ran across the ceiling and were illuminated to highlight the paintings, creating an ambiance in the room. Each wall was painted a different hue of blue that bleed into the other, giving the space a compartmentalized look and feel that complimented each installment.

Candy led me to the lightest of the blue walls, "Here's Bob's work," she said, beaming at a row of paintings.

They were oil paintings. White spattered on canvas with streaks of black and torn pieces of monopoly money shellacked randomly throughout. A few paintings had the actual monopoly game pieces glued on in 3-D.

"Bob loved monopoly as a kid. The paintings remind him of his childhood. "He calls the series, *Entitlement.*

My head cocked to one side, analyzing not only the paintings but the mind of the white man that created them. "Interesting," was all I offered up for Candy.

We experienced the other paintings in the gallery space. She talked a mile a minute about how the space doubled as her passion project and a tax write off for the partners. Most of the art was by the partners or their family members. They occasionally sold a few pieces or installed an up-and-coming artist in the space, which was also rented out for receptions.

"I got my degree in Fine Arts at Northwestern. That's where Bob and I met." Candy had lunch catered in and we were sitting in the loft above the gallery. We dined on grilled salmon and asparagus over mashed sweet potatoes with warm pumpernickel bread. A bottle of Sauvignon Blanc was perched in a gold-trimmed ice bucket, and white lining table cloth, napkins and crystal stemware adorned the table. The chunky brunette served the plates, filled our glasses with wine, and excused herself.

"I hope you don't mind that I took the liberty to order in," she said. "I thought it would give us a chance to get to know each other." She took a bite of her salmon. "Bob and I have an interest in this restaurant. Isn't the salmon delicious?"

The salmon melted in my mouth and the sweet potatoes had a tartness to it that was a nice alternative to the sweetened version Grandmama Pearl taught us how to cook at home. "Everything is so delicious. So, you and Bob have an interest in restaurants? How exciting. And you said you owned this gallery space?"

She filled our glasses with wine. "We have an interest in the gallery. We own the building that houses the gallery, the bakery, and you know, the whole block," she said nonchalantly.

My mind flashed back to the triple net seminar I'd taken. "Impressive," I said, tipping my glass to her.

"I knew Bob was going to be successful. I have this knack for judging a person's character, and there was something about him that screamed money, honey. He was the only one in the student center that was actually studying. I said to myself, he's going to be successful, and I locked in on him, and well, the rest is history."

Candy went on to spill the tea about her humble beginnings, how she worked her way through Northwestern on Pell grants and part-time jobs.

"In college, it was easy to point out the haves and the have-nots," she said. "The difference between the kids that had to claw their way through and those who had the trust fund. It seemed so unfair, but I figured instead of playing the victim, I'd use what I had to get what I wanted. So happened, that what I had, Bob wanted, and I gave it to him, honey," she laughed.

"How long have you been married,"

Candy smiled and pushed away from the table. "Sixteen years. We got married right out of college." She went behind the bar and returned with another bottle of chilled Sauvignon Blanc. "I see you have a few gentleman callers," she said, popping the cork on the wine and filling our glasses again.

"Not really," I said, not sure how much I wanted to reveal, even though I practically knew her life story by now.

"Where'd you meet Kash?" She continued to pry.

"A real estate seminar," I said, leaving it at that.

She clasps her hands together in front of her on the table. "Real estate seminar, huh? She reflected on this for a minute. "Buy land, they're not making it anymore," she said in a dramatic gesture. "A quote I heard once. Real estate is an interesting business. It can bring you great wealth or dig you so far into a ditch it'll feel like you'll never get out. When playing in real estate, discernment will be your best friend. Everything and *everybody* else, be very suspicious of."

She threw up her hands. "Oh, I forgot dessert." She jumped up and went to the serving tray left by the young attendant and returned with two thick slices of cheesecake. "Dig in." She placed the cheesecake in front of us. "It's my favorite."

She actually stopped talking long enough to eat hers in silence. She seemed to savor every bite. It wasn't my favorite dessert, but I didn't want to be rude, so I nibbled on the sweet, mushy cake while dissecting what she said about real estate. It sounded like something Grandmama Pearl would say.

We said goodbye and agreed to connect again real soon. I drove south, reflecting on her life. While my intentions were to build a possible business connection, the afternoon turned into more than that, and I had the feeling there was more to come.

CHAPTER 21

Doc checked his watch and stretched his neck down the block, looking for his Mazda RX-7.

"Later, Mr. Turner." A voice from a group of students shouted as they left school for the day.

"Y'all get home safe, now," Doc said, checking his watch again. He paced up and down the sidewalk. He had a great rapport with his students; they considered him one of the hip teachers. He'd experienced some of the things they were going through and could relate to them.

As a teen, he'd gotten into some serious trouble but escaped jail time behind the grand theft auto case he'd caught. He felt guilty because it landed his best friend in jail. They hadn't spoken since the night the cops arrested them. His friend didn't see freedom again until he completed four years on a six-year sentence, and even then, he wasn't free. Once in the system, always in the system. Doc knew now that it was designed that way for people like him. When his friend got out, Doc was so far gone having tried to bury his guilt in alcohol and drugs, that they never reconnected. It wasn't until alcoholic anonymous turned his life around that he got himself together, enrolled in college and now held his master's degree in social work.

He finally noticed the Mazda creeping toward him, it rolled to a stop in front of him, and he leaned into the passenger side window. "You're late. I've…" her glassy eyes told him all he needed. He walked around to the driver's side and opened the door. "Slide over."

"I got it," Jasmine said. "Gone get in the car."

Doc tried easing her over. "You shouldn't be driving. Move over."

Jasmine shoved him aside and shut the door. "I said I got it."

Doc didn't want to make a scene in front of the school. He walked around and got in the passenger seat. Jasmine floored the gas and the car leaped forward; she slammed on the breaks, bringing it to a screeching stop. She started laughing hysterically as students and faculty stopped and looked over at the commotion.

Doc scanned the small crowd gathering; he painted on a smile. "Teaching her how to drive a stick," he shouted out the window. He turned to Jasmine, "I got this, babe. Slide over and let me drive you around, you deserve it," he said, trying to pacify her.

She was still laughing and nodded her head at him. He got out and she climbed over the stick shift into the passenger seat, and Doc drove away.

"Damn, Jas, you said you needed to borrow the car for work."

"I did go to work. Only had a few clients today."

He shifted the car into third, "It's bad enough you're late, but high, too. Drinking and driving is not cool?"

"I told you I had to meet up with my study group. We smoked a little weed and had a beer."

"Beer. You drinking beer now?"

"That's all they had," she clapped her hands, "Why you nagging me, damn, it was a couple of beers and some damn weed!"

"Oh, now it's a couple of beers, I see. Okay, Jas. You don't need to be drinking and driving, that—"

"Stop telling me what I need to do, Doc."

"What if you have an accident—"

"Oh, you worried about your car? "

"No, I'm—"

"Mine will be out the shop next week—"

"…worried about you."

"…so, you can have your car back—"

"Forget about the car, okay. This isn't about the car. It's about you. I've been where you are and you are heading for disaster, if you—"

"Stop! Just stop with the alcoholic anonymous bullshit. I am not an alcoholic, okay!" she yelled, clapping her hands to every syllable. "That's you. What you went through, you went through, don't put that on me. I got my shit together. Got it?" She'd gone from laughing hysterically to yelling at the top of her lungs.

Doc went silent. He never engaged her when she went into her drunk rants.

"GOT IT!" she repeated. She propped her elbow on the window sill, resting her head in her hand.

They rode in silence before Doc attempted to speak again. "Just know that I'm concerned, and—"

Jasmine jerked forward and cranked the music up and started singing out loud and off-key.

Doc maneuvered through the traffic keeping quiet for several minutes before speaking again. He was waiting on the mood to change. When he felt the shift, he spoke in a calm and relaxed voice. "So, what do you feel like for dinner?"

Jasmine sat up and turned the radio down, "Hmm, that's a good question," she peered out of the window, "Oh, make a left up here. Let's stop by Sinclair's."

"Without calling?"

Jasmine cut her eyes at him. He shrugged and made the left.

They pulled up in front of Sinclair's fourplex just as Carlos and his crew were calling it quits for the day. Sinclair was standing out front looking up at her building.

"What's up, Sin?" Jasmine shouted out of the car window.

Her loud high pitch wasn't lost on Sinclair, who turned to face them. She looked at Jasmine's glassy eyes as she stumbled toward her, shook her head and looked back at the building.

"They got it off," Jasmine said. Referring to the spray paint Charmaine had tagged her building with the first night they met.

"Yup, power washed it. Hey, Doc," Sinclair said as he walked over.

"Looks good," Doc said.

"What brings y'all here?"

"In the neighborhood. About to get something to eat."

"Come on up," Sinclair said, walking inside. "I'd offer you something to drink, but I see you already beat me to that."

"Don't you start. I'm fine," Jasmine said.

"Yeah, that's what you keep saying." Sinclair walked inside.

Jasmine stood in the foyer. "Nice. It's come a long way since I was here last," Jasmine said, peeping into the unit. I love these colors."

"That's all Charmaine," Sinclair said, giving them a tour of the two downstairs units.

Charmaine had accented the white walls in the bathroom and kitchen with blue/grey tile combination. She painted an accent wall in each room to make the tile pop. In one of the units, instead of the white trim, she used a light grey trim, something Sinclair resisted at first but was amazed by the results.

Doc ran his hands over the grey woodwork, "Simple, but upscale. Looks ready to go on the market."

Sinclair took a deep breath, "Soon, very soon. Have to find a replacement, first," Sinclair said, walking up the steps into her unit.

"You won't have no problem getting rid of this," Doc said. "What's your listing price,"

"I was think—"

Jasmine laughed, "Doc trying to sound like he know what he talking about."

Doc sat down on the couch. "I know about—"

Jasmine waved her hand in his face, "You don't know, Jack," she said, plopping down on the couch next to him.

Sinclair watched as Doc took a deep breath. She was waiting on him to check Jasmine, but he let it go.

"May I use your bathroom," he asked.

"Sure, down the hall," Sinclair waited until the door closed. "Girl, why you talk to that man like that?"

"What do you care? You thought he was a gangster or something at first."

"Well, I misjudged him."

Jasmine pointed her finger toward her, "Clearly not your strong suit."

"Whatever that's supposed to mean."

Jasmine counted on her fingers, "uh, Trace, uh, Tony, uh, what was that boy's name in high school—"

Sinclair's eyes widened. "You got a lot of nerve, with your two-sheets-to-the-wind half the time."

"Look! I'm tired of everybody always talking about..." She counted on her fingers again. "I work a full-time job, carry a full load in school, hell, I deserve to relax," she shouted, jumping in Sinclair's face. "Hell, I'm grown."

Sinclair didn't move, "Girl, you better get out of my face. What's wrong with you?"

They were within an inch of each other's noses when Doc came out of the bathroom. "Whoa, Whoa," he said, stepping between them.

"I'm grown! Stay out of grown folks, business!" Jasmine yelled.

Doc gently guided her away from Sinclair. "Come on, baby. We know, we know. It's all good."

The telephone rang and Sinclair took a deep breath to calm herself before answering it. "Hello... Yes, speaking... Thanks for getting back to me. Did you find Charmaine..." She listened for a long time, a grave look covering her face. "What? Oh my God." Sinclair sat down at the kitchen table.

Jasmine, clocking Sinclair's concern, was listening. "What is it, Sin?

"Where..." Sinclair grabbed a pad and looked around for a pen to write with.

Doc pulled one out of his inside jacket pocket and handed it to her.

"Thank you. I will. Goodbye," Sinclair hung up the phone and looked around at Jasmine.

"What is it, sweetie?" Jasmine said, going to her. "Is Charmaine alright?"

Sinclair's eyes darted about the room. She breathed away the lump that had formed in her throat. She looked into Jasmine's eyes whose closeness was welcomed, unlike the heated moment they shared seconds ago. "She's in juvey. They got her locked up in juvenile camp."

"Oh no!" Jasmine said, hugging her cousin for dear life. Remembering the pain her brother Kyle's juvenile experience brought on their family. He was sent to juvey at fourteen by a judge that didn't care that he was a straight A student, and the shoplifting he was charged with was his only offense.

A talented singer, and big fan of Teddy Pendergrass, Kyle stole a forty-five by Harold Melvin and the Blue Notes, so that he could practice the song for the upcoming school talent show. A bad decision by a dumb kid who had the money to buy it, but even the Jewish record store owner said he could work it off. He was devastated that his teenage worker called the police on Kyle, but the judge was relentless and refused to exercise any leniency, instead sentencing Kyle to serve time in juvenile camp where his life took a turn down a road that he hadn't managed to get off of to this day.

On visits Jasmine's heart would sink when seeing the waiting room filled with black boys from her neighborhood. She wondered where they sent the white kids who shoplifted and committed crimes as juveniles, because there was certainty none there.

She held on tight to Sinclair, knowing thoughts of Kyle wasn't far from her mind and made a vow to become Charmaine's, biggest advocate, this black girl, that she'd unfairly judged so harshly, shared her same struggles in a world that refused to see them.

Chapter 22

anny let the phone ring; when the answering machine came on, he buried his face in the receiver and tapped it against his forehead before leaving another message. "Hey, it's me again. You got my number. Call me back, will you?"

He went back to drinking his coffee and reading the morning paper. The story had broken about Alderman Melvin Tanner. The FBI had raided his offices and the indictment seemed inevitable. Carla had heard the news east coast time and called him at the break of dawn.

"It's happening. We'll want to move fast?" Carla said.

"Morning, Mom," Danny said, half asleep. "By the sound of your voice, I'd say Tanner just got his ass handed to him."

"By the FBI themselves. I'll call Winston and set up a conference call for later today. Can you be available?"

"Do I have a choice?"

"Son, we've gone over this—"

"I know, but it's Saturday."

"Politics is twenty-four-seven."

Danny buried his head in his pillow. "Ok, whatever, fine."

After the call, he'd lain in bed staring up at the ceiling. He'd tried everything from promiscuous behavior to removing everything out of his apartment that reminded him of Sinclair, but she was still the first thing he thought about in the morning and the last thing at night. He'd called so many of his shallow dates by her name that he didn't even bother addressing women by name anymore. Since seeing Sinclair at the bakery, things had only gotten worse.

He poured himself another cup of coffee, lit a cigarette, and tossed the newspaper in the pile with the others on the floor. Normally he kept a pretty neat place, but since the break-up, he hadn't been able to focus on anything, let alone housework. Dishes towered in the sink, clothes hung on furniture, and a trail of shoes had accumulated from the front door. He was on to his next case and files and folders were strewn about the room.

The phone rang, and he snatched it off the hook. "Hello." He signed when Carla's voice greeted him.

"Danny, hold on. I got Winston on the other line." She connected the calls. "Danny? Winston?"

"I'm here," Danny said.

"Danny, my man. Winston Collier."

"Nice connecting with you," Danny said.

"Feels like I know you. Carla talks highly of you."

"That's what mothers do."

"You'd be surprised. Hey, look. There's a lot to cover. Best we do it in person. Can you get away today?"

Danny closed his eyes and wiped his hands across his face. "Sure," he finally said.

"Winston, I thought you were ready to discuss now," Carla chimed in.

"Face to face is best. Danny can fill you in." To Danny, he added, "Let's say two o'clock. You know the Cherokee Restaurant in the Loop?"

"Yeah."

"See you there at 2:00." Winston hung up.

Frustrated, Carla sighed into the receiver. "I was hoping to strategize over the phone. I want—"

"He's the campaign manager, let him manage. That's why we're hiring him, right? I got to go, Mom. I'll keep you posted," he said, hanging up the phone before Carla could say anything else.

He was used to Carla's controlling nature but never noticed until recently how it dominated his life. Growing up, it was just the two of them. She was always there for him, from cub scouts to baseball, he never felt neglected. Most kids' fathers weren't in the picture, so Danny actually felt proud when his mother was the one parent that did show up. Her schedule was always planned around his events and he'd gotten used to her being in his life and appreciated the guidance and direction she provided. For the women he dated, who thought his mother's involvement in his life was too much, he'd chosen his mother every time. But now, choosing Carla over Sinclair felt like a bad choice. He didn't think a short-term Alderman seat was a bad idea; he just hated the way he went about trying to convince Sinclair. He could have taken a much different approach, and jumping down her back about taking a day to herself, for whatever reason, wasn't the best way to lead into that conversation. He figured if she would just talk to him, he could make it right and convince her to come back.

The morning hours flew by as they often did as daydreams of reconciliation dominated his mind and his time. He ran through the shower and purposely, as an act of defiance against his mother, dressed down for his meeting with Winston, putting on jeans, Jordans, and his favorite Members Only jacket.

The weekend traffic in the loop was lighter than during the week, filled mostly with tourists instead of the downtown workers in their week-day grind. He found a parking spot and walked the few short blocks to the restaurant. It, too, was empty, except for a few stragglers. Not seeing Winston, he picked a spot in the back, facing the door and ordered a cognac on the rocks.

At two o'clock on the dot, a man in a grey fedora, and a blue Izod shirt over grey dress slacks tailored to his medium build frame, strolled in. It dawned on Danny that he had never met Winston in person. He nodded at the stranger as he made his way toward Danny's booth.

"Danny Boone?" the man asked, stretching out his hand.

Danny stood, accepted his handshake, and the two men took a seat.

"You're just like Carla described. Except I wasn't expecting the Jordan's."

Danny shrugged. "Weekend wear, you know."

"I hear you. Nothing wrong with keeping a low profile," Winston said, signaling for the waiter.

"If that can be done in Chicago in two-hundred-dollar Jordons."

The waiter made his way to the table, "Let me have a bourbon, neat, and another one for him," he said, grabbing the menu from the cradle, "and let me have the special." He held the menu out for Danny.

"Special sounds good," Danny said.

Winston moved from small talk to business with the ease of a career politician. "This is what we're dealing with," he said, propping his elbows on the table and talking with his hands. "Now that the Feds have raided his office, it's just a matter of time before they push your office, U.S District Attorney, for indictment. That's where you come in, or better put, where you go out. Can't have you working on the team that indicts him and attempting to be appointed to his seat."

Danny nodded. "Makes sense."

"No law says you can't work there until we get everything lined up, but in no way, whatsoever are you to have anything to do with the indictment."

Danny considered this. "The only way that works is if I let my boss know I have my eye on that Alderman seat."

Winston leaned back in the booth. "Got no problem with that, do you?"

The waiter brought their drinks back to the table. "I can think of a few problems," Danny said, pouring the remainder of his old drink into the new one. "Never mind, it looks like I'm taking a step down in my career. When he asks why I'm taking that step, and I tell him it's to run for Chicago's District Attorney—"

"Naw, naw, naw, you don't have to tell that white boy all of that. Look, never put all your cards on the table, number one. See, this is why you meet in person, all of the nuances don't come out over the phone. Number two, who says it's a step-down?

Danny realized he was echoing Sinclair's words. She was adamant that his status as a federal prosecutor trumped a Chicago City Alderman, and he kind of agreed.

Winston continued, "Politicians make moves in their careers all the time and granted, you're not a politician yet, but you soon will be. Your federal prosecutor title may sound glamorous, but you're not getting to DA for the city of Chicago from there. As an Alderman in this town, being appointed to that ward, everybody knows your name. When it's time to run for the DA, that's what you want. And that's where the power is, not from some peon federal prosecuting trial attorney job."

"Thanks a lot. But check this, though. As federal prosecutor, I might get assigned Tanners case, and that will put me on the mind of the people in this city—"

"You think they're going to assign a big case like that to a junior prosecutor?" Winston said, leaning in. He took a swig of his bourbon as Danny contemplated this.

Winston answered his own question. "No. But put your experience as a federal prosecutor and an Alderman against a candidate for DA, I'd bet on you."

The waiter appears with the tray of two specials and set the plates of baked chicken and mashed potatoes in front of the two men. Danny was beginning to sink into the idea of his appointment as Alderman and ultimate run for District Attorney.

"So, who's my competition," Danny asked.

Winston sliced his chicken breast, "Nobody we have to worry about. Some white cat the developers are pushing to be their yes man. Which is exactly what you want to avoid at all costs. It's the reason Tanner is in the mess he's in. We run a squeaky-clean campaign and an even cleaner office once you're in. You tarnish your reputation with a federal probe of any kind, and you won't be able to get arrested in this town, let alone another job in the legal field."

Danny lifted his drink, "To squeaky-clean!"

Danny took the long way home and found himself in front of Sinclair's fourplex. Signs of construction underway were gone, as was the graffiti sprayed by Charmaine. Sod had been laid and bushes planted and a for sale sign stood in the front yard. Danny sat there feeling a bit left out. He was supposed to be celebrating this milestone with her. Sinclair had talked about investing in real estate from the early days of them being together, and he was happy for her and sat there wondering how they had drifted away from supporting each other in their dreams.

High on his meeting with Winston and with a greater understanding of how the Alderman seat could be good for him, Danny summoned up enough courage to knock on the door. He got out of his car and stood across the street, watching to see if there were any signs of anyone inside. Sinclair was the only occupant of the building and he couldn't tell which apartment she was in now that they had all been rehabbed. It was still light outside and hard to see if there were any lights on inside. He crossed the street and made his way up the walkway toward the door. The door leading into the foyer was locked and he peered into the window to see what he could make out.

"Danny!" The voice came from behind him.

He turned around to face Sinclair. He clocked the white man in an Armani suit and Stacy Adams but held a poker face. "Hi, I was, you know—"

Sinclair glared at him, "No, I don't. What are you doing?"

He looked at the white man. "Can we talk in private?"

Sinclair sighed, "This is not a good time, Danny."

Danny shifted from side to side and stuck his hands into his Members Only jacket. "It'll only take a minute."

Sinclair rolled her eyes and turned and walked back down the walkway toward the street.

Danny followed, walking past the white dude, making sure to give him eye to eye contact. When he and Sinclair were out of earshot, he spoke to her in hushed tones. "The place looks great."

"That's not why you're here, I'm sure."

Danny ran his hand over his hair, "Um, like I was saying when I saw you at the bakery, I mean, ever since then, I can't, I mean, I think about you all the time. Did you get my messages?"

Sinclair looked away from his eyes, "I did."

"Can we talk? He said, pausing for her response. When none

came, he pleaded his case. "We never really talked. It just kind of ended."

"And I remember exactly why it did. And nothing's changed." A heavy silence lay between them. "I'm sorry. I have to go." Sinclair hurried back down the walkway toward Kash, who was waiting.

"Sinclair," Danny yelled. "Sinclair, can't we talk?" Desperation washed over him. "I love you."

Sinclair kept moving forward until she stepped inside and raced up the stairs. Kash stood in the doorway, peering back at Danny through one eye, before shutting the door and following Sinclair upstairs.

CHAPTER 23

I watched Danny as he walked back to his car. His, *I love you* buzzed in my ear like tinnitus, but weighed heavy on my heart. I pushed the emotion away and instead relied on my head. He had shown me who he was. "I'm over you," I whispered as he drove off.

I heard Kash come in behind me. "You good?" he asked.

"Yup!" I plastered on a smile and swung around to face him. He'd come to see the fourplex. It was about ready to be put on the market. "Let me show you the other units," I said, grabbing the keys from the hook on the kitchen wall.

We walked through the units and Kash eyeballed the detailed work, "Real nice. Quality craftmanship. Great color scheme," he said, looking around the space. "Nice job for a rookie. Should sell quick."

"It was an experience for sure, but God is good," I said.

"All the time," Kash said, on cue.

I returned the praise. "All the time."

"God is good." He was smiling. "A church girl, huh."

We walked back to my unit. "Born and raised. My grand-mamma did not play. We were in church every Sunday."

"Man, you don't have to tell me. My Pops was a preacher."

My feet froze on the steps. "No way. You a PK? You didn't tell me that."

"It's complicated," he laughed.

"I bet it was. A black preacher with a white first lady?"

"Naw, she wasn't around. Stepmother raised me. She black."

It hit me that I didn't know a lot about Kash. We talked the day we met about him being mixed, but since then the conversations leaned toward real estate development and Chicago politics, which he was convinced worked hand in hand.

We made our way back to my unit. "Any siblings?"

"Got a half-brother," he said. "Moved to Los Angeles, trying to break into the music business. Sang in the choir at church."

"Can I get you anything?" I asked. "Have a seat."

"He sat down on the couch, his legs open in that male-dominance-taking-up space kind of way, "That's a loaded question, girl."

I rolled my eyes, "Let me be clear. Can I get you something to drink?"

He grinned. "Sure, I could use a cocktail. Surprise me. Turn on some music."

"I packed my albums up but got some nice cassette tapes over there on the shelf."

As Kash flipped through the cassette tapes, I opened a bottle of Rum and splashed it over ice, adding more coke to my glass than his. My mind drifted to our conversation about church. It had been a while since I'd attended. I felt bad, guilty, really. During the hard times, when I found myself in that walk through the wilderness, I was in church every Sunday. Praying for God to help me overcome all the difficulties I was dealing with. He showed up in a big way bringing multiple people into my life, from Trace to Danny, to Tony, and while those relationships didn't turn out in the best way, each one provided me with what I prayed for. From the job I got exactly when I needed it because Trace came into my life, to the financial gain I made because of knowing Tony, to the love Danny provided when I needed it the most. God was there, right on time. It seemed the more my hopes and dreams came to pass, the less time I had to spend on God, and that was bugging me and had to change.

"You know they have something called CDs now?" Kash said, bringing me back to the present.

"What?"

He popped a cassette into the player. "CDs. Stands for Compact Discs. The music industry is moving toward that new technology."

"No way that's replacing albums." I placed the drinks on coasters and sat down on the couch. "No way."

"That's what they said to the Wright Brothers. 'No way that shit's gonna fly'." He popped in the tape and joined me on the couch.

"I get it. I'm all about technology; worked in it. Got a degree in Mass Communications—"

"Then you should know. Times are changing. We either get on board the train or get left behind. He lifted his glass, "Toast. To change, the one constant thing in our lives."

I thought about how constant change described almost every relationship I had in my life, from my father dying when I was eight years old, my mother having a break down not being able to care for me, to the men in my life that had come and suddenly gone—Trace by death, Tony by crime. There was no abrupt change that pulled Danny and me apart. It was a slow process that seeped into our lives while we weren't watching and hit us with a dose of reality. That's why I couldn't understand why he was back. Couldn't he see that we weren't right for each other?

Kash was grooving to the music and enjoying his rum and coke.

The fact that he was comfortable in the silence between us was a welcomed trait and why I like hanging out with him.

"I really like this jam," he said as Luther Vandross's voice drifted through the room.

Kash began to sing along to Luther and I was floored by the tone of his voice. He sounded like an angel was singing to me. He lifted me from my seat and led me in a slow dance as he continued to sing in my ear. I relaxed into his arms and enjoyed the touch of a man—something I hadn't had in weeks. The song finished and we released our embrace.

"Damn, you got it like that?" I said. 'Boy, you can sing. I mean, really—"

Kash pressed his lips to mine. In my mind, I was resisting, but my lips kissed him back. We stood there pressing our bodies together, the touch of his skin creating a warming sensation through my blood. Danny kept clicking on and off in my mind, and I kissed Kash harder, trying to cancel him out. We found our way onto the couch, where I lay on top of him, still locked into the kiss that had taken control of us. I was completely lost in the moment, it was like someone had cast a spell on me and I sank deeper and deeper into his power, but in my mind's eye, it was Danny's body I was touching, and Danny's scent I was smelling. When I felt his hands slide down my pants, the spell was broken and I leaped up from the couch and backed away.

"We can't. We're friends."

He laid there looking up at me, clearly aroused. "I don't kiss my friends like that," he said, adjusting his pants. He sat up on the couch and gulped down the Rum and Coke, holding the glass out to me.

I took his glass and mine. "I think we've both have had enough," I said, taking them into the kitchen.

"What you running from?"

"Nothing," I said, returning and sitting in the chair across from him.

"You thinking about that ball and chain."

I sucked my teeth and dismissed him with a wave of my hand. "You tripping."

He chuckled, stood up from the couch and stretched. "I gotta bounce. I'll check you later."

I stood and walked him to the door. "Ok," I said, then tugged on his lapel. "We're friends." Trying to convince myself as much as him. "You're going to be my real estate buddy."

Kash studied every inch of my face as if he'd seen it for the first time. Then looked me square in my eyes. "I'm gonna be your man," he said, kissing me on the forehead before walking out the door.

The phone rang before I had a chance to fully process what he said. I answered it, and the social worker that was helping get information on Charmaine spoke in hushed tones. Instead of discussing the news over the phone, she asked if I could meet with her. I made the appointment and hung up, a bit curious about what would be said in person that couldn't be said over the phone.

CHAPTER 24

Tina stepped off the elevator and down the hall toward the flickering naked light bulb. She knocked on the door of her father's apartment.

"Use your key," the voice from inside shouted.

She dug in her purse and pulled out her key and let herself in.

Sitting in his favorite chair in front of the television, Odell yelled at the contestant on the screen. "Dummy, I knew that was a zonk from here."

"Daddy, I picked up some Chinese Food for Dinner tonight."

"That's okay, baby, Chinaman's fine," he said, not taking his eyes off the screen.

Charmain took the food out of the bag. "I can't eat with you tonight. I got to meet Sinclair. Where's Stanley?"

"Said he gone to see a man about a job."

Tina stopped in her tracks, "What kind of job?"

"Didn't say." He threw his hands up. "The box, take the box!" he yelled at the screen.

"Where's the TV tray, "Tina asked, looking around the kitchen.

"Stanley got it in there in his room, I think," he said, lifting himself out of his chair, and shuffling to the bathroom during the commercial break.

Tina went into Stanley's room. She was amazed by how everything was in order. The bed made was made with the sheets and spread tucked neatly into the mattress. He kept his toiletries on the dresser in a neatly arranged line and his two pairs of sneakers were lined up in the closet, with the laces tucked inside. She spotted the tray on the other side of the bed and went around to get it stumbling into a shoebox that was on the floor next to the tray, and kicking the top slightly ajar. She looked toward the door to check to see if her father was still in the bathroom. Seeing the coast was clear, she bent down and picked up the box, placed it on the bed, and removed the top. She pulled out photos and letters she and others had written him in prison. Prison photos of him, other inmates and their visitors in the signature prison-kneel pose in front of a concrete wall with a painted backdrop. There was a paperback copy of Claude Brown's, *Man Child in the Promise Land.* The pages dog-eared like he marked his favorite parts. She kept digging past more photos and came across a newspaper clipping at the bottom of the box. It was yellowed and faded, but the September 1970 date was clear, and the headline read, *Remains Found in Cabrini Green Trash Shoot.* She stared at the headline, trying to process the words. She wasn't sure why her heart was racing but was shaken from her prying by the sound of the front door opening. She shoved everything back into the box and hurried out of the room and down the hall, just as her father was heading out of the bathroom. She pretended to help him to his seat, knowing he hated being treated like he was an invalid.

"I got it. I ain't crippled. Where my Chinaman at?"

"I'm getting it now. Hey, Stanley. You hungry?" I bought you some Chinese food," she said as Stanley was digging through the bag.

"I can eat," he said.

Tina placed the tray of egg foo young and fried rice on the tray and set it in front of Odell. "You can eat here in front of the TV today, Daddy. I gotta go."

"Where you off to?"

"I told you to meet up with my friend, Sin."

"Sin? What kind of name is that for a girl, Sin. Is she a sinner?" He got tickled and couldn't stop laughing.

Stanly started laughing with him.

"Real Funny. Wash your hands, Stanley. I gotta go," she said, heading out the door.

"To meet the sinner?" Odell yelled, behind her, laughing with a mouth full of fried rice.

Tina hopped into her car, removed the wheel lock and made her way to meet Sinclair. The headline from the faded newspaper clipping was on replay in her brain, *Remains Found In Cabrini Green Trash Shoot.*

"Remains in a trash shoot," she whispered. "That's crazy. I don't remember that, and why was Stanley saving that clipping?"

She parked her car and made her way inside the DCFS building, where Sinclair was waiting in the lobby.

"Thanks so much for coming," Sinclair said, rising to greet her.

Tina gave her a hug. "No problem, I got you. You sounded freaked out on the phone."

"The social worker freaked me out. Talking about we needed to meet in person,"

Tina frowned. "What the hell is going on she can't tell you over the phone?"

"Exactly."

A petite woman with a Jheri curl walked through the door and up to Sinclair. "Ms. Ellis."

"Nice to see you again, Vicki."

"If only under better circumstances," Vicki said.

Tina folded her arms, "Better circumstances not a part of your job description."

Vicki held out her hand to Tina. "I'm Vicki Summers, and you are?"

"A good friend of mine," Sinclair answered. "You had me so worried. I expected the worse and wanted her with me in case the news was—"

"I wish I did have better news. Come with me," Vicki said. Instead of walking back through the doors toward her office, she led them outside to the sidewalk. "I'm afraid Charmaine's detention may not have been…" she searched for the right word. "…random."

Confused, Sinclair looked at Tina and then back at Vicki. "Meaning?"

"That she was set up?" Tina said, agitated.

"I'm afraid she's right. It seems Mrs. Grey, the social worker who took over some of my files, has a history of placing youth from South Chicago into mostly white northern communities like Deerfield to—"

Sinclair caught on. "Set them up for failure?"

"Nine times out of ten, the youth don't adjust well, one bad incident in the home or school, and they're—"

"Placed in the foster care to prison pipeline," Tina said. "I saw it growing up in the Greens every day."

"What's in it for this Miss Grey?" Sinclair asked.

Vicki sighed. "More and more youth camps are privatized now. Since the war on drugs campaign—"

Tina threw her hands up. "Camps my butt. They're jails. Prison for kids."

Annoyed, Vicki walked away from the building. "Look, I agree.

I'm on your side. That's why I'm telling you this. I believe Miss Grey is taking kickbacks from the youth camps administrators in exchange for bodies."

Sinclair stopped walking. "She's getting paid to incarcerate black kids."

"I don't think she discriminates," Vicki said.

They made their way to a small pocket park. Tina paced back and forth. "So, what are you doing about it?" Tina asked.

"I don't know how far up the chain this goes. It wouldn't be wise for me to take this to my boss. Which is why I didn't want to talk over the phone."

Sinclair nodded. It made sense now.

"I know your fiancé is a federal prosecutor. I thought perhaps you could have him look into this. It could be pretty widespread. If Miss Grey is doing this, there could be others, and a federal probe could go a long way."

Sinclair squeezed her head between her hands. She didn't want to get into her and Danny's breakup with Vicki. "I'll see what I can do. In the meantime, can we get her out?"

Vicki bit her lip. "It's not my case anymore, and once the youth offend, they're harder to place in family homes."

"Can she go back to the group home?" Sinclair asked

"I'm afraid not back to Sherri's. It's a non-offender home. Now that Charmaine has this on her record, she'll have to be placed in an offender home or an approved foster care home if she beats her case and doesn't have to serve time.

"Record? Serve time. Are you kidding me?" Sinclair said,

"Oh man," Tina added.

"A juvenile record. It'll be sealed once she turns eighteen," Vicki said.

Tina shook her head in disagreement. "The charge will be, but the arrest won't. She'll forever have to check the box that she's been arrested," Tina said, remembering her brother's juvenile records that resulted in prison time for each of them.

"What exactly did she do?" Sinclair wanted to know.

"Threw a book at a student who called her... let's just say a derogatory name, I don't use that word. I would have wanted to throw a book at him, too." Vicki pulled out a folder from under her coat. "Here's a list of all the youth assigned to Miss Grey who ended up in juvenile camp. There's a number in there to reach me if you or Danny need anything else."

Sinclair took the folder. "We've got to get her out of there."

Vicki nodded and squeezed her hand. "I'll see what I can do."

"No! We're getting her the fuck out of there!" Sinclair shouted. "This is some bullshit!" She and Tina marched down the street, clearly on a mission.

CHAPTER 25

Real Estate agents come a dime a dozen. The key is finding a good one with your best interest at heart instead of lining their own pockets. The agent who helped with the purchase of the four-plex was just seasoned enough to have gained savvy negotiating skills but not in the business so long that she was inflexible and arrogant about her real estate knowledge. When I find a good product or service, I like to stick to it, so I called the same agent to list my property. Building a team around me that I could trust was important for the future deals I had on the horizon.

Today was our first open house, and I'd gone through the property with a fine-tooth comb. We had staged one of the units to give buyers a welcome home feeling. The housing boom was in full swing by 1986, and we set the listing price aggressively, agreeing that the property would be a good investment for an owner-occupied buyer or an investor who wanted to buy and rent. Every angle was covered with the goal of getting the highest offer in the shortest amount of time. Homeowners were looking to take advantage of the lower interest rates and tax shelter created by the Economic Recovery Act before the other shoe fell. I remember one thing Tony taught me in our long talks about economics, 'It's all cyclical, Sin. Get in, keep your eyes on the exit door, and know when to get out.' I was all in.

Out the window, I saw the realtor drive up. She lugged an open house sign from the car and stuck it in the yard, attaching balloons to it. I met her at the door. "Good morning, Ava," I said, not hiding my excitement.

"Hi, Sinclair. It's a beautiful day for an open house," she said, carrying several bags through the foyer and into the staged unit. She placed the bags on the kitchen counter and spun around, checking out the room. The stager we used was her connection and we were both pleased with her work. I thought of Charmaine and how she would have loved to be a part of the staging process; adding her flair to it could have only made it better.

"Everything looks perfect," Ava said as she began to empty the contents of the bags on to the counter. "I picked up some refreshments. I use it to entice buyers to hang out a little longer. The more people milling about, the more they get the feeling of competition. Everybody wants what they think other people want," she said, arranging Danish pastries and fruit on a tray.

This is why I liked her, always thinking. She removed cookie dough from her bag and began rolling the dough onto a cookie sheet.

"The smell of fresh cookies makes the place feel like home. I want to stimulate all the senses," she said, taking a tape recorder from her bag and popping in a cassette tape as smooth jazz filtered through the air. She adjusted the volume placing the music just below the surface.

I smiled, "You got this. Do your thing. I'll be back later. We can talk about some of the open houses I've been checking out, so when you sell this one, we can pounce on the next one," I said, grabbing a Danish.

"I've got pouncing down to a science," she said, placing the cookies in the oven.

I swept my arm across her spread, "That's obvious."

I headed out to my car, but the signs of spring ushering in the Chicago summer enticed me to walk the few blocks to my destination. I headed toward the Hyde Park business district past bungalows and apartment buildings where a kaleidoscope of flowers in bloom danced in the warm Lake Michigan breeze and filled the air with a delicate flora scent. I walked down East Fifty-third Street, past the small businesses and shops that lined the block, and saw Kash standing in front of the restaurant.

For him, he was dressed down in a crisp white shirt that he wore open collar and untucked over a pair of Calvin Klein jeans. I loved the suits he wore but was equally impressed with this casual look. I'd always envisioned myself in a corporate job, where I would get decked out in designer suits and high heel shoes, but plans have a way of turning on us, forever reminding us who's really in charge. Instead, I landed a job at Kahn Telecommunications as an installer wearing a uniform and work boots, and now as an independent real estate investor, I change my look to suit the occasion. While there were times when a suit was in order, I mostly enjoyed the upscale casual but comfortable attire I'd adopted for myself.

Kash smiled at me when he spotted me coming down the sidewalk. It was like our near romantic encounter never happened, and I was glad he was able to not sweat it. The more we spent time together, the more I liked his business style. He used his racial ambiguity to his advantage in a form of modern-day *passing*. Unlike our ancestors of the past, Kash could care less if it was discovered he was black by those who did business with him because they thought he was white. As far as he was concerned, the joke was on them. Judging a book by its cover created limitations for the judgmental person but opened up a field of opportunities for the misjudged. In the real estate business, where everything was built on racial covenants, redlining and other discriminatory practices, Kash had figured out how to exist in the space between the two worlds to benefit his objective.

Happy to see each other, we embraced and he led me into the restaurant, past the hostess table without stopping and into a back room where people were already gathered. I followed Kash past the fully-stocked buffet and to a table where several men were seated drinking and smoking cigarettes. I made out Bob and Candy past the haze of smoke that billowed above their heads. I hadn't seen Candy since our luncheon.

"Candy! Hi!" I said.

She didn't return the same over-the-top enthusiasm. The bubbly personality displayed during our gallery lunch had morphed back into the doting wife, more seen and not heard.

"Bob," I said, more even keel after getting the cold response from his wife.

"Sinclair! Nice seeing you again." His enthusiasm matching mine. "How's that four-plex coming along."

"All done. Just left the realtor at the first open house," I said, my enthusiasm returning.

"Open house?" he said, holding his cigarette hand suspended in the air.

"Yeah. So, I can look you up when I'm ready for my next one, remember?"

Bob puffed on his cigarette, "Indeed I do," he said, pausing to blow smoke in the air. He turned to the white man sitting next to him. "Selling? In this neighborhood. Now?" he whispered, but not low enough that I didn't hear him, before turning back to me. "What's your listing price?"

Before I could answer, someone tapping silverware against a water glass brought the room to attention. I sat there a bit discombobulated. I turned to look at Kash to see if there were any non-verbal cues, but he was engaged in a conversation with another man before the tapping silenced the room, so I wasn't even sure he'd heard Bob's snide remark.

"Gentleman... and ladies," the speaker said, tipping his head toward the table where Candy and I were seated. I scanned the room and realized we were the only women there. "Welcome to the Chicago Developers Coalition. Given the recent news of the FBI raid on the offices of Alderman Melvin Tanner, we thought it prudent to call this emergency meeting."

Scanning the room again, I recognized some of the folks from the developer's reception Kash had taken me to, although now peppered with a few more black men than seen at the reception.

"The petition is going around and we're going to need each and every one of you to sign it. It's calling for Tanner's suspension in light of pending allocations and indictment against him—"

"Isn't that kind of premature," someone yelled from the room.

"No, no, I don't believe it is, and the board of directors is with me on this. We have heard from a very reliable source that it's just a matter of time before the indictment is issued and we want to be ready."

"What's your plan?" someone else wanted to know.

"Glad you asked," the speaker said, lifting his hand toward the back of the room. "Hunter, come on up here."

The young man Kash pointed out to me at the reception, as the developer's choice for Tanner's seat, walked up to the front.

The speaker continued as Hunter took his place beside him. "Hunter here has been an attorney in my construction business for a few years now, and has been instrumental in working with the city on everything from building and safety to planning and zoning, to sanitation, you name it. He knows this city government inside out, and furthermore, he owns property in Tanner's ward and is our choice to replace him so that we can have an ally on the city council that understands our needs."

Approval from the crowd rippled through the room. The men passed the petition around as Hunter took center stage. He wasn't much older than me, his cocky demeanor boosted by the privilege he'd been afforded his entire life and the selected ignorance toward having it. He muttered a few empty phrases about helping to bring integrity back into the ward when he's appointed Alderman and pushing for the tax incentives and variances needed for developers like them to build up the blighted areas of the south side of Chicago.

"We can give these people a life they can be proud of," he had the nerve to say.

I listened with a straight face, playing my cards close to my chest like Trace had taught me, and noticed that Kash had his poker face on also. I heard Candy smirk and looked around at her. She was wearing her disdain on her sleeve and I couldn't wait to find out what that was all about. It was clear that I was dealing with a Dr. Jekel and Mr. Hyde, depending on if her husband was present. I remembered our discussion about her humble beginnings and wondered if that had anything to do with the split personality I was witnessing. When the petition got to our table, Kash and Bob scribbled their signatures on it, and Bob slid it across the table to Candy. When he turned his back, she looked over at me and I gave her a look, and she passed it on to the next table without signing it herself. We looked at each other and smiled.

The speaker wrapped up the presentation, hard-selling everyone to sign the petition. I decided to take advantage of the buffet.

"What balls," Candy whispered, catching up with me at the buffet table.

I was confused by her on again, off again personality, so I held my comment, switching the discussion to something non-political. As we moved down the buffet line, I noticed Kash and Bob in deep discussion. Kash adjusted his defensive body language when he noticed me watching and forced a smile my way.

We left the restaurant, and I accepted Kash's offer to drive me home. His Mercedes Benz was polished to a spit shine and glistened in the sunlight.

"Nice ride. I want to be like you when I grow up," I said.

Kash didn't come back with one of his normal witty remarks. He half smiled and opened the passenger door where I sank into the leather interior that caressed my body, and the smell of pine incense tickled my nose.

"Bob didn't seem to think selling the four-plex was a smart move," I said, looking for his expert opinion, but Kash's mind was clearly somewhere else. His brow wrinkled and he clutched the steering wheel so tight his knuckles turned red.

"Hello," I said, glancing at him sideways.

He looked at me like he forgot I was sitting there.

"You good," I asked.

"Everything's cool,"

We rode the rest of the way in silence. He pulled up to the curb, said a haste goodbye, and drove off before I could get out of the car good.

I stood on the sidewalk, looking at him speed away. It was obvious that everything was not cool but decided I had enough problems of my own.

Ava had locked up and left a note that the open house was a success. I couldn't get out of my mind what Bob said to his colleague about my decision to sell. From everything I'd researched, buying low and selling high was the strategy I needed to get to my ultimate goal of investing in bigger developments. Sure, Hyde Park had its advantages, but my image of being a landlord was rooted in my experience with Uncle Ervin and I knew I didn't want the hassle of collecting rent from working-class people. I was clear on the risks in all of it, but I wanted to focus on the bigger risks that brought bigger gains. Unless there was something I was missing, selling the four-plex was a sacrifice I needed to make to reap a bigger reward. I kept telling myself that, but Bob's words were haunting me.

A glass of wine and reading a good book sounded like a good way to end the hectic week I'd spent finishing the final touches of the rehab and getting ready for the open house. I popped the cork on a bottle of Pinot Noir when the flashing light on the answering machine caught my eye. Jasmine left a message wanting to know if I wanted to hang out tonight, "No," I said out loud, pressing delete. The next message was from Ava, asking if I got her note, reiterating the successful open house, and letting me know she'd call me later. "Cool, cool," I said, deleting the message and pouring wine into the glass. Then, Danny's voice echoed from the machine.

"It's me... Ah, I... call me back... We need to talk... seriously, is that it? We're walking away, after all we've... look we can work this out... just call me back, okay."

I hit replay and listened to the message again and again as I sipped my wine. The tone of his voice reminded me of the early days with him before Carla wedged her way into our lives. His plea for me to call him back touched the deepest part of my soul where I had buried my love for him. I had already decided I needed to talk to him, but not about us. I wanted to discuss if he could help with Charmaine, but was waiting until the open house was behind me.

Now that it was, I picked up the phone and dialed his number. He picked up on the first ring.

"Sinclair?" he said.

"Gotta love that new caller ID," I said. "The beginning of the end of privacy in this world."

"Thanks for calling me back," he said.

"I need—"

"Let's meet. Talk in person, and—".

"I need a favor," I said.

"Anything," he said without hesitation.

"It's Charmaine."

The silence that followed was expected. I let it lay there between the phone line, forcing him to respond.

He finally answered. "Believe it or not, I've been... I mean... Well, I'm sorry about the things that I said about her. You were right; she's just a kid, and your helping her is no different than the concern you showed for my siblings. I was jealous. If you'll just let me show you, give me another chance. I'll make this right."

A deep sigh rose from the pit of my throat. I didn't want to deal with what Danny was feeling right now. His guilt would have to wait, he'd shown me his true colors, and Grandmama Pearl always said, a leopard doesn't change his spots".

"She'd appreciate that," I said. "That you're sorry, but right now, she could use your help."

I relayed the story about her being in juvenile camp, about Vicki, the social worker that helped us with Trevor and Josh, and the story she shared about what looked like a foster care to prison pipeline. "If you could look into that. Maybe see if we can get her out on a prison-for-profit technicality or something until the investigation or probe or whatever y'all do, is complete. I don't know; I'm just trying... I have some documents I can share that Vicki gave me."

"Sure. Don't worry. How about I stop by and pick them up tomorrow. See what we got and what can be done to get her out—"

"I'll drop them off at your office on Monday," I said, cutting his attempt, to get into my apartment, at the knees.

I needed it to be clear, if not to him, to myself, that he was just a means to an end—getting Charmaine out of the clutches of the penal system.

CHAPTER 26

"Thanks, Tina, you put your foot in this brunch," Jasmine said, pouring more champagne into her glass and adding a splash of orange juice,

"I do what I can," Tina said. "Cooking for my three brothers and daddy, growing up, I learned a little something, something."

Sinclair lifted her glass in the air, "Toast to Jasmine getting that MBA."

"And to Tina for finally letting us in her crib," Jasmine said.

"That's what I'm talking about," Sinclair said. To Tina, she added, "Took you long enough. What was that all about anyway?"

Tina cleared food from the small table she'd set up near the window. It was really a part of the living room, but she had repurposed the space so that she could have an area to entertain *him* for dinner. The small one-bedroom apartment was a mansion compared to the projects she was coming from, but Sinclair and Jasmine were way ahead of her when it came to having a nice crib to call their own.

"It was nothing. Just needed to get it together. Y'all living in high rises and buying fourplexes and stuff. Nothing fancy about this place," she said, placing the coffee cups she'd gotten from Sinclair's goodwill box on the table. "Y'all want coffee?"

"Another mimosa for me," Jasmine said.

Sinclair and Tina exchanged glances.

"I'll take some coffee," Sinclair said, looking around the space. "I actually like what you've done with the place. Come on give us the nickel tour."

"More like a penny," Tina said.

"Girl, stop putting yourself down like that," Jasmine said, getting up and waving her hands around the place. "This is progress."

Tina smiled. "Well, this area is the living room, kitchen and dining room. I put the couch in the center to help kind of mark the spaces off," she said.

"It works. Too bad Charmaine's not here. She could give you some pointers. That girl's got a natural talent for decorating a space," Sinclair said.

"How's she doing, by the way," Jasmine said, peeping into the bedroom that was directly off the living room.

Sinclair hadn't told Jasmine about her connecting with Danny to help out with Charmaine. She'd dropped off the documents to him, and he told her he'd get back to her once he had some news. "Danny's looking into it," she said.

Jasmine spun around, "Say what?"

"That's right. They talking," Tina said, grinning at Sinclair.

"Only on the phone and only about Charmaine," Sinclair said, taking a glance into the bedroom. It was modestly decorated with a bright pink bedspread, and pictures and other knick-knacks Sinclair recognized as items from her goodwill box. She felt bad she hadn't offered the stuff to Tina first when noticing the rug by the bed looked familiar as well. It was then she spotted them. "Wait a minute. What are these?" she asked, rushing into the room and grabbing a pair of men's shoes that were sticking out from under the bed.

Tina rushed from the kitchen, "Get you some business," she said, reaching for the shoes that Sinclair held high above her head out of Tina's reach.

"What we got here?" Jasmine said, joining the fun.

Sinclair tossed a shoe to Jasmine, who tossed it back as Tina ping-ponged back and forth between them, jumping up, trying to catch the shoes.

"Give me the damn shoes, y'all. Right the fuck the now," she yelled at them.

Jasmine stopped, concerned. "Oh, we're sorry. We were just kidding around," she said, handing the shoe to Tina, "Here you go."

Tina reached for the shoe and Jasmine snatched it back, "Psych!"

Tina grabbed Jasmine around the waist, and Sinclair tried to get the shoe, and they tussled around the room, competing for the shoes until they collapsed entangled in each other on the bed—all three of them laughing hysterically.

"Tina's got a boyfriend, Tina's got a boyfriend," Jasmine teased out of breath.

Sinclair laid on her back, clutching a shoe to her chest, heaving from laughter, "Who's the secret lover, Tina?"

Tina rolled over on her knees and looked down at her friends, laughing boisterously until suddenly morphing into agony as words erupted from her mouth in sobs. "He's married. I couldn't tell y'all who he is. I wanted to, but, but, but," she sobbed, still on all fours.

Shocked, Sinclair sat up on the side of the bed easing Tina off her knees, as Jasmine jumped up and grabbed a roll of toilet paper from the bathroom.

"Did he hurt you, sweetie?" Jasmine asked, handing her a wad of toilet paper.

Tina blew her nose, "No. he's… no… nothing like that."

"Why the secret?" Sinclair asked, sitting next to her, rubbing her back as Jasmine sat on the other side of her.

"It should have never happened. I was… he was a client. He was on my route to install cable in his office, and well, he was flirting… I might have been flirting too, we were talking about cable service, and you know, one thing led to another, and he kissed me—"

"You went from talking about cable to kissing?" Jasmine said. "How the hell—"

"Did you want it to happen?" Sinclair asked, thinking of her own experience.

"Just some random dude kissed you!" Jasmine added.

"Yes… to both. I mean, yes, I think I wanted it. He was cute and funny and—

"Married!" Sinclair and Jasmine said in unison."

"I didn't know that at the time. We actually started dating after that. Kind of, I mean, he comes by—"

Jasmine threw her hands up. "For a booty call!"

Sinclair shot Jasmine a side-eye. "We're not judging."

"He told me later that he was married. He owns a large commercial custodial business, and a lot of his contracts are with the city that he got working with that Alderman that's been in the news—"

Sinclair raised an eyebrow, "Tanner?" she asks.

"Yeah, that's the one. He helped him get a lot of the contracts he has, you know, and based on what he told me, some of them may not be, you know, copacetic—"

Jasmine rolled her eyes. "You think?"

Sniffling, Tina continued. "—and now that the FBI is after that Tanner guy, Rodney, that's his name Rodney, thinks they're going to come after him." Tina said, sobbing again.

Sinclair rubbed her back. "Don't cry. You're not involved in any of his business dealings, are you?"

"No, but he's so stressed out over this alderman dude, and I don't want him to get into any trouble. He's been so nice to me, helped me get this place, and... I was just about to ask him if he could give my brother Stanley a job. He even gives me money... then that alderman's office got raided."

Jasmine looked around the shabby chic apartment. "Gives you money to do what?"

"You know, get my hair, nails done, stuff like that," Tina said.

"Girl, you screwing a married man; he better be doing more... Ouch," Jasmine said as Sinclair reached around and pinched her on the neck. "That hurt."

Sinclair pointed her finger at Jasmine. "We're not judging. I certainly can't. Been there, done that. I'm not proud of it, but you got to do what you got to do."

"But Trace wasn't married," Jasmine said, rubbing her neck.

Tina nodded. "She's right, but I didn't know. I didn't know until I was in too deep. I've been wanting to break it off, but I don't want to kick the man when he's down. Plus, he doesn't come here just for sex. He really likes me. I like him. Besides, he and his wife don't have sex, he said."

Jasmine rolled her eyes. "They all say that."

Sinclair nodded. "I'll have to agree with her on that." She took Tina's hand in hers. "Look, relax. I'm sure Rodney, or whatever his name is—"

"Rodney Lynwood. Lynwood Custodial Services," Tina said smiling, "That's how he introduced himself to me the day I installed his cable."

"—Rodney Lynwood will be just fine," Sinclair said, smiling

back at her. "Let's just have another glass of champagne and everybody just relax.

Jasmine jumped off the bed and headed to the kitchen, "I'ma need something stronger than champagne after all that."

"This is supposed to be a celebration. I didn't mean to take us there," Tina said, following Jasmine into the kitchen. "I can't wait to see you walk across that stage next week, Jas."

"You and me both," Jasmine said, turning on the stereo and tuning in to their favorite radio station. "Don't forget, Doc is planning a big dinner after the graduation. We gonna party like it's 1999," she said, dancing to the music blaring from the stereo.

"Wouldn't miss it," Sinclair said. "Any of your cohorts invited?"

Jasmine stopped dancing in mid jig. "Girl, no, but we are planning a little gathering tonight. Still need to maintain a professional relationship. You know, in case any of them land in a position to hire me as a consultant."

Sinclair laughed, "I know that's right. It's not what you know, it's who you know, and that ain't nothing but the truth."

Jasmine searched around the packed Rush Street bar looking for the familiar faces from her MBA cohort. Out of the corner of her eye, she saw arms waving frantically in the air and recognized the classmate that asked her about her "Bo Dereck" braids. Plastering on a smile, she maneuvered through the crowd.

"What's up?" Jasmine yelled over the loud music.

"So glad you could make it," her classmate said. "Grab a beer; it's on Brad," she said, tipping her bottle toward one of the instructors they shared.

Jasmine gave her a thumbs up and elbowed her way to the bar.

"Vodka on the rocks, splash of orange juice," she yelled across the bar when the bartender acknowledged her.

Loud rock music played from a jukebox and patrons played darts in an area toward the back of the room. The lack of a dance floor didn't stop a couple from carving out a space between bar tables. They waved their hands around and danced offbeat to a noisy rock song. Jasmine got her drink and headed back to her group. The spot wasn't conducive for the networking that she'd come to do. She had avoided her cohorts as much as possible during the two-year program but had shown up enough for study groups to scope the ones who would go far in their careers. Besides being white and privileged, they possessed the looks and swagger corporate America liked to hire and promote. If the Management Consultant firm she was starting was going to go far, she needed friends in high places.

They stood around holding their beers and cocktails, yelling over the music at each other, nodding their heads like they could hear what each other was saying. With each round, they all began to relax and get a little looser and less inhibited. Jasmine had set a limit but lost track of the drinks that kept coming her way. When folks started dancing in the middle of the crowd, she knew that was her clue to get out of there.

She swaggered through the crowd, holding onto tables to keep her balance, as she stumbled her way to the door. Once outside, she took a deep breath and blinked several times, trying to focus her vision, before shuffling one foot in front of the other, her body swaying down the sidewalk toward her car. Using the hood of the car to steady herself, she opened the door and plopped into the driver's seat, her head crashing into the headrest. She squeezed her eyes shut for what seemed like a few minutes before snapping on her seat belt, finding the ignition with her key, shifting into drive and accelerating into traffic.

Jasmine wrapped her hands tightly over the steering wheel and hunched her body forward, pressing her face practically to the windshield. She blinked rapidly, trying to focus on the road, but white headlamps blinded her vision. Cars whizzed past her blaring their horns as she drove toward the lights, before a loud bang sent her tumbling, flipping over and over and over, before colliding with something that brought the car to a loud crash. Jasmine, suspended upside down in her car by her seat belt, tasted the blood in her mouth before everything went black.

CHAPTER 27

The ringing phone woke me from my nightmare. They had been coming more and more frequently even though I was attending my therapy sessions regularly. Dr. Bello suggested I take up meditation, but I hadn't been able to find a time slot to add meditation to my already overflowing schedule.

"Hello," I said into the receiver with a bit of attitude, noting the digital clock illuminated three-fifteen a.m. The words spoken back to me slapped the sleep out of my eyes and sprung me to my feet. I ran around the room in circles, searching for clothes and shoes to put on.

"I'm on my way," I screamed into the receiver, hung up, and called Tina.

I parked my car across two spaces and rushed through the emergency room door and up to the nurse's station.

"Jasmine Wade," I shouted at her. "She was in an accident."

The nurse checked a stack of charts in front of her at a pace that defied the emergency of the situation.

"Is she okay?!" I demanded.

"You are?" the nurse asked.

"I'm her cousin. Sinclair Ellis, her emergency contact. They said she—"

"Yes, she's here in surgery. If you'll have a seat, the doctor will come out to speak with you once she's out."

"Surgery?! What happened, what—"

Tina appeared at my side, "I got here as quick as I could. What's going on?"

I couldn't speak. Everything hit me at once—the nightmares, the therapy, the four-plex, my failed wedding, Danny, Carla, and now Jasmine all erupted in my gut, up my esophagus, and out through my mouth in a stream of vomit, just missing Tina, and splattering all over the floor. The nurse leaped into action, wheeling a gurney to me and lowering me to sit. She grabbed water from a nearby fountain and rolled me into an empty patient station behind a flimsy blue curtain.

Tina threw her hands in the air. "Will someone please tell me what's going on?"

I was shaking now; it was like my whole body was under attack. "Jasmine was in an accident. She's in surgery now," I said through trembling lips.

"What the... When? Where? Surgery, oh my God! How bad is she?"

The nurse repeated the information about the doctor letting us know once out of surgery.

"How long is that?" Tina asked.

"It's hard to say," the nurse said, handing Tina the water and returning to her station.

I curled myself up in a fetal position on the gurney, rocking back and forth like a baby lulling itself to sleep. I thought of the day I'd met Danny in this same hospital and suddenly longed for his calm demeanor displayed that day. I tried to imagine life without Jasmine. She'd been a part of my life since the day I was born. The bond we shared was stronger than sisters. She was the brave one that finally stood up to Uncle Ervin, stopping his abuse. She was the one that would come to my rescue when kids teased me in school about my mother. It was Jasmine that kept money on Kyle's books and let me live at her place without a job or money to contribute to the bills when I first moved to Chicago. She was my inspiration, excelling in a demanding job and carrying a full load at graduate school. Losing Jasmine would be like losing an arm.

Tina sat in the chair next to the bed with her head in her hands. Jasmine had accepted her with open arms, the two of them building their own bond that strengthened the sisterhood I held with them both.

"You okay?" I asked her.

Tears pooled in the wells of her eyes. I scooted over on the bed and she took the cue and climbed in next to me. Facing each other, we clasped our hands together, and I began to pray. I didn't know if He'd listen to me. I was all, 'please God, please' when broke and jobless, but hadn't found my way to the inside of a church or even bent my knees in prayer since things turned around for me. I'd made the excuse of being busy, which sounded like a pathetic one at the moment, but I needed God to hear me today, so I asked for forgiveness and then for him to save Jasmine; she has so much life to live.

We must have dozed off and were awakened by a middle eastern woman in a lab coat. I opened my eyes, squinting into the sunlight that was now streaming through the window. I looked around, still half asleep, as the room came into view. "Jasmine," I said, springing up, remembering where I was and why I was there. I shook Tina awake.

"Good morning. I'm Dr. Biswas. I performed the surgery on your," she referred to the chart she was carrying, "cousin, Jasmine Wade."

She paused, and my heart sank. "How is she?" I asked.

"Is she okay?" Tina said.

The doctor sighed and clutched the file to her chest. "We were able to reset her broken collar bone and stop the internal bleeding. However, she suffered a lot of trauma, and the amount of alcohol in the system made it—"

"Alcohol!" Tina said.

"Miss Wade had forty percent over the legal limit of alcohol in her system."

"Oh my God, no. Did she hurt anyone?" I asked.

The doctor narrowed her eyes, "Not this time," she said, adding, "We're required to report alcohol-related accidents to the authorities. They won't be able to take her into custody as long as she's under my care. But as soon as I think it's safe to release her, they will arrest her. She's stable now. I'll allow you a short visit."

Tina and I both rose to follow the doctor.

"Family only," Dr. Biswas said, looking at Tina,

"She's like family," I said.

The doctor was relentless, "I'm sorry. Strict hospital policy."

The worried look in Tina's eyes made my blood run cold. I hugged her, "Keep praying. She's going to be alright."

I followed the doctor down the corridor, the flicker and buzz of the florescent lights casting an ominous feeling over the already gloomy night. My heart skipped a beat when I saw Jasmine through the ICU glass before entering her room. My legs wanted to move forward, but my brain shut down and wasn't cooperating with the messages my legs were sending it. I stood paralyzed by the tubes protruding from her body, her head encased in bandages, the only sign of life coming from the blinking lights of the machines surrounding her bed.

Seeing my reaction, Dr. Biswas's eyes softened for the first time. "She's in good hands," she said.

Her concern released my brain and propelled me forward into Jasmine's room. The sound of the machines beeping around her was the final confirmation that my cousin had come within an inch of her life. The tears stung my eyes and flowed freely down my face. I took Jasmine's IV taped hand in mine and gently squeezed it, hoping that He had heard my prayers.

CHAPTER 28

Kash pulled the Mercedes into the circular driveway and stepped out onto the immaculately landscaped grounds of lime hydrangeas and purple salvias. He scurried up to the eight-foot mahogany entry door of the stately Tudor Revival, where the brick, tile and limestone exterior glistened in the glow of the moon. A Mexican woman in a maid's uniform welcomed him into the living room with mile-high ceilings and massive windows to match. He chose a seat by the fireplace, flanked on either side by built-in bookshelves.

"Mr. Bob will be right with you," the maid said before disappearing into another part of the majestic structure.

Kash straightened his tie and cuff links and wiped an imaginary smudge off of his Stacy Adams. He crossed his legs, then uncrossed them sitting up straight, before leaping from his seat and pacing the floor, stuffing his hands in his pockets. He was anxious. Tanner's indictment had been announced just this afternoon, and the Chicago Developer's Coalition was moving into position to get the city council to appoint Hunter Forsythe.

"Kingsley," came a voice behind him.

Kash spun around to see Bob, dressed in a smoker jacket and

holding a snifter of brown liquor. He plastered on a smile and, like an autopilot, adjusted his dialect to fit his audience. "Good evening, Bob."

Bob walked to one of the built-in shelves and pulled down a cabinet that revealed a full bar. "Drink?" he asked?

"I'll have what you're having," Kash said, taking a seat by the fireplace.

Bob poured from a bottle of Remy Martin XO and handed it to Kash, neat.

Kash savored the cognac, licking the nectar from his lips. "Can never go wrong with this," he said, studying the liquor in his glass.

"Yes, you seem to enjoy the finer things in life," Bob said, taking a seat by the fireplace across from Kash. "If only you could afford them," he said, crossing his leg over his knee and swirling the liquor in his glass.

Kash shifted in his chair, dismayed. "Bob, you know I'm good for it."

"What I know is what you've demonstrated, and the investors are not happy with what they're seeing. Not happy at all."

"We just need a little more time. Once the ordinance is passed, we can complete construction—"

"You are out of time."

Kash threw back his drink in one gulp. "It was a bad loan to begin with, and you knew—"

"You knew the terms. You came to me with your ill-planned pipe dream. Not a bank in town would take that deal. We turned you down and you shuffled and jived your way into a hard money loan. Don't twist it like you didn't know what you were getting into."

"Tanner swore he could he get the ordinance passed."

"The only thing Tanner's getting is time in a federal prison cell.

It's your neck on your line, and I am not going down with you. I used my contacts to get you that loan, and they want their money."

Kash exploded out of his seat, "My hands are tied here, Bob. The construction is stalled, and my partners don't see a way out unless we can get this zoning ordinance passed. This Hunter kid is our only chance. We get him appointed to council and it's a done deal."

"Even if we do, it won't be in enough time to save your neck. You're eating hard money interest every single day. You've got to stop the bleed."

Kash slumps in his chair.

Bob pours himself another cognac and sips it slowly, watching Kash stew. "My partners and I may have a possible solution for you," he said, leaning in.

Kash mirrors his lean.

"That young lady with the property in Hyde park."

"Sinclair?"

"It's on the market, right?"

Kash nods, not sure where this is going.

"Set up a dummy LLC; tell her they're developer friends and broker the deal to purchase from her.

Kash laughs out loud, "Purchase with what?"

"Albright Savings and Loan will approve a mortgage to the LLC. We'll make sure it looks real good on paper. In exchange, we'll cure the debt you owe in arrears, until you can get Hunter to vote in the ordinance."

Kash reclined in his seat, contemplating. "Why not just buy it yourself?"

"We'll buy it from you, at a lost to the LLC, of course. You get the tax write off, we'll get the property under market value. Our goal is the whole block. It won't look kosher for a group of mortgage bankers to be buying up blocks of residential property, so we've set up a REIT.

"It's a low rent residential. What would you want with property on that block?"

It backs the commercial district. That zoning ordinance passes, it's rezoned into prime commercial property. Worth ten times her listing price."

Kash frowned and shook his head. "I don't know. If the property is going to be worth ten times its current value, she'll want to know—"

"What she doesn't know won't hurt her. She's got it listed anyway, right? You'll be the hero bringing her a buyer. Tell you what, offer her ten percent over asking. She'll think she hit the jackpot. Or, you can deal with my partners. I must warn you they're not as reasonable men as me."

Kash knew a threat when he heard it. He didn't know exactly who Bob's investors were, but he knew the hard money Bob loaned him wasn't on his Savings and Loan books. There were rumors that the Albright Savings and Loan family had ties to the Chicago Irish gang, but he hadn't been able to substantiate it and didn't think this was a good time to find out. Kash bit his lip and took a deep inhale. "She is selling anyway. Ten percent over asking, huh?"

Bob nodded.

"Tell you what," Kash said, his energy returning, "cure not only my arrears but also restructure the loan from hard money to conventional, and you've got yourself a deal."

Bob hesitated.

"Hey, I'm taking all the risk here. You're asking me to commit tax fraud, foreclosure, and god knows how many other violations." Kash said.

Bob sat back in his seat, his eyes shifting back and forth, before landing on Kash, "Deal," he said, hand extended.

Kash grabbed it, thought about it. "And if Hunter Forsythe doesn't get the appointment to the city council?"

Bob squeezed Kash's hand in an iron grip, "It's in your best interest, that you make sure he does, or you've got a problem that I can't fix."

CHAPTER 29

O pened fire hydrants, packed beaches and humidity that drenched the air signaled that the hot days of Chicago's summer had arrived. Danny wiped the sweat from his brow and tossed his cigarette out of the car window, waiting like a detective on surveillance again. He hadn't realized how much he'd missed this part of law enforcement. As a federal prosecutor, it had its perks, but he missed doing the leg work. The part that put the pieces together and solved the crimes. This made the prosecutor's job seem like a walk in the park.

He flipped through the notes he had gathered on the juvenile cases he'd gotten from Sinclair. In three months, Miss Grey had placed forty-nine kids in foster care. She'd transferred them from thriving inner-city group homes to majority-white communities where most floundered in the unfamiliar surroundings. Minor school infractions, from skipping class to Charmaine's book throwing incident, violations that earned the suburban kids a few days of suspension, landed the black foster kids in juvenile camps.

Danny spotted Miss Grey exit the Department of Family and Children Services building. He hopped from his car and jockeyed across the street. "Ellen Grey?" he said, catching up with her in the parking lot.

Alarmed, she stepped back, "What do you want?"

Danny raised his palms. "I just have a few questions." He stepped slightly forward.

"Don't come any closer. I'll scream," she said, clutching her purse.

Danny was used to the biased treatments received from white women. The combination of big and black seemed to trigger an automatic threat to them. The multiple degrees and prestigious law position were no contest for a perceived frightened white woman.

"Great, we can tell the cops all about the forty-nine black kids you placed in juvenile camps. Listen to the screams those kids have."

Miss Grey shifted her eyes around the parking lot, "I don't know what you're talking about." She marched around Danny.

"These tell me otherwise," he said, flipping through the files. "Charmain Willis, thriving at Calumet group home, transferred to Deerfield, Nathan Brown, Lisa Franks—"

Miss Grey spun around. "That's not public information. Where did you get that?"

"I'm asking the questions here. And you either answer me, or I can get a search warrant and we can investigate your entire department."

"You're a cop?"

"I'm the person with all the information I need to put you behind bars for a very long time," Danny said. He let that sink in and watched as a new kind of fear wiped over her. "But, I'm sure you're not working alone. First person that talks, walks?"

Miss Grey's light brown eyes darted about. Perspiration stained the armpits of her polyester suit that suffocated her under the noon-day sun. She wiped the sweat-drenched, dirty-blond hair off her forehead, her hands shaking like jelly. "Everyone's doing it," she blurted out.

"Doing what?" Danny said.

"I mean," she threw her hands up, "That's our job. We take them from undesirable homes—"

"Not this one. She was a straight-A student in a group home rated one of the best in the city, but you snatched her out," he said, pointing his finger in her face. "You sold her for profit to a juvenile camp like chattel, and you'll do the time—"

Her eyes widened, and terror spread over her face. "It wasn't just me. At first, it was just kids that were going to end up in the camps anyway. So—"

"So, you thought you'd give them a little push. Make a few bucks on the side while you're at it."

"They said the camps would be good for them. Make sure they went to school, keep them off the street. They said—"

"Who is they?"

Miss Grey trembled. "Very powerful people," she said, shaking her head. "They approached me. Knew my husband was sick. That my house was in foreclosure, and we needed the money. All I had to do was sign over a few kids to the camps... I'm so sorry. I didn't mean to hurt anyone."

"I'm going to need names," Danny said.

Miss Grey told the grueling details of a foster care to prison pipeline. From the caseworkers and judges who railroaded the youth into the system for pay to the probation officers and juvenile camp administrators who kept them there to feed the pipeline, a privatized prison system made possible by Regan's phony *War on Drugs* rhetoric.

"Will you be willing to make a formal statement?" Danny asked.

They had sat down on a nearby bench in the shade where Miss Grey recounted the stories of her involvement with a chain of officials who were a part of the elaborate scheme.

"First to talk, walks?" she asked.

"It will certainly put you in a better position than your co-conspirators," Danny said, rising from where they were sitting.

Miss Grey rose with him. "Can we get them released?" she asked, following him to his car. "The kids out of those camps?"

"It's prison, Miss Grey," he said, opening the car door. "You put children in prison in exchange for money."

She hung her head and slid into the passenger seat.

Horns blared in all directions as if that would ease the gridlocked traffic Danny was stuck in on the Dan Ryan. He wished he had taken Lake Shore Drive to Sinclair's place, but in his excitement to tell her the news in person, he'd hopped on the ramp to the freeway, and it was too late to turn back now.

Ellen Grey had dropped a dime on everyone from her immediate supervisor to a juvenile judge that was also on the take. Caseworkers got paid to turn the kids over to the courts, and the judge got paid to sentence them for minor infractions to feed the privatized camps that got paid by the county for the number of youths they housed. Everyone's hands got greased at the expense of a black child's life.

Danny thought about his little brother, Trevor, and how he could have easily ended up in a camp making a group of investors rich while he rotted behind an iron door. Trevor's mother had fallen victim to the crack epidemic, and Trevor bounced back and forth between his mother's apartment and his grandparents. After Trace died, Trevor was left to fend for himself until Danny united with him and was able to get him in a nice foster home.

Danny sat in traffic thinking about his brothers, Trevor and Josh, two of the sons Trace left behind. Had he not met Sinclair, his brother's fate would have been in the hands of someone like Miss Grey. He inched his car forward, cringing from the reality that inner-city neighborhoods all over America were having the life choked out of them because of the crack epidemic. The President and the white ruling class had waged war against the neighbor-hoods and the people in them instead of treating it like the health crisis it was. Chicago's south side had been hit hard, and parents were getting swept up in the drug trade and leaving in its wake a reservoir of innocent black children that the system warehoused like property to line their own pockets.

His dreams of him and Sinclair adopting his two youngest brothers flooded back at him. He was still in love with her and the distance between them was wearing on him. He secretly hoped that his news about Charmaine would make her just happy enough to remember how much he loved her and would do anything for her. Carla was a problem that he was willing to deal with, if it meant getting Sinclair back in his life.

Spotting his exit, he eased over to the right and made his way off the freeway and through the streets. Evidence of the drug trade was made clear by the corner boys he passed along his route and the blighted areas that lacked grocery stores, shopping centers and any sign of commerce until he hit the Hyde Park district, where Chicago Police flooded patrols to protect and serve the white stu-dents and faculty of the University of Chicago, while leaving the rest of the south side of Chicago to fend for themselves.

Danny found a parking space near Sinclair's and jetted down the sidewalk and up the walkway to her building. Surprised that the entry door was unlocked, he entered with caution, taking two steps at a time up to her apartment. "Sinclair," he yelled, banging on her door. "It's me. You okay in there?" He waited for a response. When none came, he banged again, and finally, the door cracked open.

Sinclair's red and swollen eyes peered through the crack in the door. "Why are you here, Danny?" she said, half-asleep.

"You okay," he asked, sensing something was off. "You gonna let me in?"

Sinclair sighed.

"I have news about Charmaine," he said.

Sinclair opened the door and stepped aside, letting Danny in. A blanket and pillow were strewn on the couch. She ran her hands down her body, trying to smooth out her rumpled and wrinkled clothes. "I fell asleep on the couch," she said.

Danny looked around the darkened room. He knew this woman like the back of his hand, she wasn't a middle-of-the-day napper. "What's wrong, babe," he said, calling her babe on autopilot. He saw the tears well in her eyes. "What is it? Is it your, Mom? What—"

"No, it's Jasmine," Sinclair said through the uncontrollable sobs. "She's in the hospital from a car accident. Tina, Doc and I are taking turns—"

"Whoa. Slow down, slow down," he said. Not fighting the impulse, he embraced her in his arms. "Car accident? Jasmine?"

"She's in bad shape, Danny. She's in real bad shape," she said, melting into his chest.

"Shhh, don't cry. I'm sure she's going to be alright."

"I don't know, I don't know. On top of everything else, she was driving drunk. Police are just waiting for the doctor to release her, so they can arrest her."

Danny absorbed this news. Chicago PD was out of his

jurisdiction, but he still had friends on the force. "Did she hurt anyone?" he asked.

Sinclair shook her head, "No, thank God."

Danny sighed, held her arm's length, and assured her. "I'll make some calls."

Sinclair nodded and wiped her face. "Thank you," she sniffled.

"I got you," Danny said as someone knocked on the door.

Kash stuck his head in. "Hey, door was open—" He stopped once he noticed Danny behind the door. "You okay, Sin?"

"I'm fine except for all the unexpected visitors?"

Kash shrugged, "I stand accused, but with good news."

She sighed, "I could use all the good news I can get right now.

Kash rubbed his hands together, "I got a buyer for the property," he said, smiling, before noticing her tear-stained face. "You sho you good?" he said, giving Danny a side-eye.

Sinclair shook her head. "Jasmine's been in an accident," she said.

"Ah, man. I'm sorry about that. Wishing her a speedy recovery," he said with prayer hands. "Look, I can have that offer over to you tomorrow."

"I'll talk to Ava about scheduling a showing?"

Kash smiled. "Told the buyers all about it, they good. Offering ten percent over asking," he said.

Danny looked at him sideways.

"I'll have Ava contact you," she said.

"Name's on the sign out front. I can call her to get the deal going—"

"She said she'd have Ava call you," Danny said.

Kash looked him up and down, "Man, I'm not talking to you."

Danny stepped to him, "I'm talking to you. Man!"

Sinclair, distressed, "Really? Stop it, just stop it. I got enough going on." She turned to Kash. "Ava will call you tomorrow. Good looking out."

"You know I got you," Kash said, glaring at Danny. "We'll talk tomorrow."

Danny closed the door behind Kash. "I don't trust that joker, Sin."

Sinclair waved her hands at him. "Danny. Don't."

Danny wanted to go there, but he was just getting back on her good side, so he let it go for now.

"I gotta shower. My shift is up next at the hospital," Sinclair said, opening the door for Danny.

"I'm going with you," Danny said, taking a seat on the couch. "She's my friend too."

Sinclair held the door open with one hand, the other hand on her hip.

Danny crossed his legs. "Besides, if the doctor releases her, you'll want me there when they come to arrest her."

She looked at him and closed the door.

CHAPTER 30

The rhythmic sound of the ventilator pumping air into Jasmine's lungs lulled Tina in and out of a restless sleep. She opened her eyes to the clock on the wall signaling that Sinclair would be there soon to bring her takeout and relieve her of her duties. They had kept a twenty-four-hour watch around Jasmine since her accident. Dr. Biswas had assured them that she was stable and her unconsciousness was a normal reaction to the brain trauma she had suffered.

Tina massaged her temple between her thumb and index finger, thinking about the massage Rodney promised her when she got home. She'd let Lincoln know she needed vacation time and found him unusually accommodating. Generally, he was a complaining pain in the ass, but when she told him her friend had been in a car accident, he went soft on her and told her to take all the time she needed.

She stood up and leaned over Jasmine's bed getting nose to nose. "Hey, Jas," she whispered. "Please wake up." She squeezed her friend's hand, sat back in the recliner, and grabbed the Jell-O that food service had left on the tray, peeled back the foil, and slid the sugary treat into her mouth with the plastic spoon. So much was running through her mind. *What would happen to Jasmine? Who would care for her if she couldn't take care of herself?* Tina wasn't sure if she was a natural-born caregiver or had been forced into the role when her mother left. Still, the thought of people being alone with no help made her anxious. As a young girl in a house full of males, she often felt alone and isolated. Her only relief was when she busied herself with cooking, cleaning and caring for others so she wouldn't have to think about the hole in her heart left by her mother abandoning her.

A long time ago, her mother left, but tears still stung her eyes when she thought about that day. Before she left for school, her mother had fixed them oatmeal with cinnamon and raisins and hugged them all before they left. She remembered how pretty she looked in her pink sweater that buttoned down the front and grey plaid skirt. The way she smiled at Tina before she left for school that day was forever burned into her memory. So, when her mother didn't make it home from work that night and wasn't there the next morning, or the next, Tina always envisioned that pink sweater and grey plaid skirt one day walking back through that door, but the day never came. She often wondered if she liked cooking for her family because that was the last thing her mother did for her.

The door opened, and Tina was shocked but secretly happy to see Danny walk into the room with Sinclair. "Look what the cat drug in," she said, getting up and greeting Danny with a hug. "She's still the same," she whispered in Sinclair's ear while hugging her.

"Has Dr. Biswas been in to see her?" Sinclair asked.

"Not since Doc left this morning, but the nurses have been taking good care of her."

Danny stood next to the bed. He took in the room and all the equipment surrounding Jasmine and inhaled, the air escaping his lips with a slow nervous breath. He looked at Sinclair and Tina,

"I'm so sorry, y'all. I'm going to make a few calls to see what I can do about the DUI charge against her. It's worth a shot."

"Now that's what I'm talking about," Tina said. "That's why you associate with folks in high places. Them ghetto rats can't do nothing for you."

Sinclair shook her head at Tina, smiling for the first time since the accident.

"Which reminds me," Danny said. "I never got to tell you about Charmaine."

Sinclair snapped her finger, "That's right. Kash came by and—"

"Oh, oh, Kash came by?" Tina cocked her head at Danny. "While you were there?"

Danny nodded.

Tina threw her hands up, "You gotta wake up, Jas. You missing all the fun."

Sinclair laughed at her friend, then looked at Danny. "Charmaine. What's up with that."

Danny clapped. "A rainbow in the midst of a storm," he said. "We got a confession from the caseworker. She sang like a bird to save her own neck."

"Does that mean Charmaine is coming home?"

Danny's face lit up. "A few minor details, but yes. I think we can make that happen,"

Tina and Sinclair grabbed each other and started twirling like schoolgirls playing Ring Around the Rosie.

"Halleluiah!" Sinclair shouted.

"Hell yes!" Tina screamed. They were basking in the joy of the victory they both needed. Doing a little dance around the room and high fiving each other, until suddenly the machines keeping Jasmine alive went haywire, interrupting their celebration.

BENG! BENG! BENG! the buzzer rang out on the ventilator,

the lights on the machines surrounding Jasmine's body began to blink like lightning bugs, nurses emerged into the room and a voice over the intercom shouted, "Code blue, cold blue," over and over.

"What's happening?" Sinclair screamed in horror. "What's happening?"

Dr. Biswas appeared, as a nurse ushered them out of the room into the hall, drawing the curtain around Jasmine's body so they couldn't see.

Sinclair beat her hand on the glass, "Open the curtain! OPEN THE DAMN CURTAIN!" she yelled before her body went limp, fainting toward the floor, caught by Danny just in time as he swept her up into his arms.

"I got you," Tina said, as Sinclair opened her eyes.

"Danny?" Sinclair called out. She was lying on a gurney in the hallway outside Jasmine's room.

"I'm right here," he said, taking her hand.

Sinclair relaxed at his touch, then sprang straight up, "Jasmine!"

"They're still in there," Tina said, just as Dr. Biswas opened the door to Jasmine's room.

Tina sat on the gurney next to Sinclair as Danny stood by, holding her hand.

The three of them tracked Dr. Biswas's steps as she walked toward them down the hall. She stopped and addressed Sinclair.

"I'm afraid she's taken a turn for the worse,"

"No, no, no," Sinclair wailed. Danny put his arm around her, bracing her for more bad news.

"She's slipped into a coma, and—"

"You said she was stable," Sinclair cried.

Dr. Biswas took a deep breath. "Whenever there is trauma of this magnitude, anything can… There was a chance this could occur. We had stabilized her, but the swelling in the brain caused her to slip into a coma—"

"For how long?" Tina said. "When will she wake up?"

"It's hard to say exactly. Most patients are awake in a few days or weeks."

"Weeks?!" Sinclair moaned.

"We'll do everything we can," Dr. Biswas said. "Constant stimulation helps. Talking to her, massaging her limbs. Do you have other family members who can help? The more she's stimulated, the better. Try not to worry too much." The doctor laid her hand on Sinclair's shoulder. "Patients wake up from a coma and in most cases resume normal activity."

The doctor disappeared down the hall as Sinclair's cries bounced against the white tile walls and echoed in the distance.

CHAPTER 31

I thought about Dr. Biswas's question about my family members and realized that all Jasmine and I had were each other. The remaining family was my mother, the mentally ill, Uncle Ervin, the child abuser, and Kyle, the convict. I hadn't gone to see my mother since my last year of college. The experience was so traumatizing I hadn't been able to return until now. I'd kept in touch through letters and phone calls and communications with her doctor but suddenly had an overwhelming urge to see her, to be by her side. I only hoped that I had picked a good day for her when the medication, group sessions, and the demons that haunted her were all on good behavior. I just needed to see my mama as I remembered her as a little girl—less all the crazy.

Her doctor had reported that they'd managed to craft a drug cocktail that seemed to be working. For years, the side effects of the medication they administered seemed to do more harm than good, making visits with the family disastrous. In the early days, her doctors thought my mother being institutionalized would be temporary, so they prescribed at-home weekend visits to acclimate her back into the home environment. I would set up my tea set in the room I had at Aunt Mattie's and Uncle Ervin's house, anticipating her arrival. She'd start out all smiles at first, but the first sight of Uncle Ervin or one of my father's other brothers would send her spiraling into an uncontrollable schizophrenic episode.

Walking down the corridor of the mental hospital, not much had changed through the years. Even the front desk receptionist was the same red-haired woman with glasses. The only change was the blue-framed cat-eyed glasses she wore were updated to more stylish frames.

"Hello, Miss Ellis," the receptionist said, her bright smile and cheery voice juxtaposed to the dreary room. "Your mother is so excited about your visit today," she said.

"She knew you were talking about me? I asked.

Deja vu swept over me, the friendly exchange oddly familiar from my last visit that took a turn for the worse when my mother imagined me to be my father's mistress and violently lashed out at me. The orderlies had to carry her out screaming and kicking. Her face and body twisted in a fiendish contortion that haunted me for months after.

The receptionist pushed her stylish glasses up her nose and handed me a pass. "Keep this with you. We had to start a new policy when one of the patients strolled out with the visitors one day." She shrugged. "Just like that, gone."

"Oh no," I said, alarmed. "Were they found?"

She waved the matter away with her hand. "Oh yes, of course. Didn't get farther than the parking lot. Realized it was fried chicken day for lunch and wondered back in on his own. But we don't want that to happen again," she said, her robust laughter echoing through the room.

I managed a smile and studied her face, wondering how she maintained such a cheerful disposition in such a gloomy place. Then out of the blue, I said out loud, "In God's presence, there is the fullness of joy."

"What was that, dear?" she asked.

I didn't know where that came from. I looked at her like a deer caught in headlamps, frozen for a split second, wondering if God had just spoken through me. It had been a while since I'd heard from Him, but I knew enough to know that it was because I hadn't been listening. "Nothing," I finally said. "Is my Mom in the dayroom?"

She nodded and pointed down the hall, her smile never leaving her face.

I walked down the corridor toward the day room. A pretty name for a room where they placed the patients, regardless of the time of day, to live out their trivial lives in oblivion. It overlooked the grounds of the institution, where other patients wondered about in full conversations with themselves or staring off into space. Orderlies in white uniforms were positioned throughout the grounds, ready to correct any unacceptable behavior.

I was happy to see that the dayroom, like the receptionist's eyeglasses, had received an upgrade. The drab grey furniture had been replaced with a bright flora design and matching yellow drapes. The stark white walls, now painted in pastel colors with matching flora wallpaper borders that ran the circumference of the room. Someone had given some thought to the décor, right down to the high traffic carpet, while not plush, was pleasing to the color palette.

I scanned the room looking for my mother, but she spotted me first, and I heard her call my name. The sound of her voice jerked me back to my childhood memories of cooking dinner together, reading bedtime stories, or when all three of us would walk over to Uncle Ervin and Aunt Matte's on warm summer nights, where they'd play bid whist under the big cypress tree, while Kyle, Jasmine and I played hide-and-go-seek, or caught lightning bugs in a jar. I turned toward her voice to see her standing in a bright orange summer dress by the window. She was smiling at me, and it felt like my feet left the floor and floated to her, taking her up in my arms.

"Mama. I've missed you so much," I cried into her hair. It smelled like her favorite hair dress that I sent in her care packages every month. "I'm so sorry that I haven't been here—"

My mother grabbed my cheeks in her hands, her eyes searching my face. "Mama was sick, but I'm better now. Don't you fret yourself." She led me over to the flora couch. "Sit down, and tell me all about it. I've been having dreams about you. You still going to church?"

I lowered my head, but she lifted my chin. We were in church every Sunday as a family, the entire Ellis clan. Daddy's brother Uncle Coltrane was the pastor, and everybody knew the Ellis family that piled into the fifth pew on the right side of the sanctuary every Sunday morning. The ushers would quickly usher any visitors who didn't know better to another seat.

"You lift your head, child. There's no shame in not going to the church house from time to time. Life gets you down that way, but in God's presence, there is the fullness of joy," she said, her eyes piercing my soul.

My mother and I shared a bond in that we both had premonitions. We could feel something was about to happen before it did. I'd experienced it many times, but my mother's gift was exceptionally strong. The night my father died, she felt it, and I'm certain that knowing it was going to happen and not being able to stop it is what drove her over the edge. I had to come to terms with that with Trace. I knew there was something wrong. I felt it in my bones, my spirit spoke it to me, but I couldn't do anything to stop it. Maybe that's why I've not listened to God ever since. I don't want to hear about any tragedy that I don't have the power to prevent. I know that you blame yourself when that happens. I hope my mother finally realized that what daddy did to cause his untimely death was not her fault.

Mama rubbed her hands through my hair. "Remember when I used to braid your hair?"

Blushing, I nodded. It was growing back and was in an in-between state, too long for my pixie cut and too short for a bob.

She twirled the ends around on her fingers. "Can I braid it now?" she asked.

The kid in me giggled and slid to the floor between her legs. Handing her a small comb that I kept in my purse, she parted my hair and began to cornrow it.

She insisted I talk to her about everything I'd been doing. The doctor had suggested that I not agitate her with bad news, so I skipped over the bad stuff sharing the purchase of my first property, Tina's acceptance in college, wedding planning, and Jasmine's upcoming graduation. And while these things hadn't turned out the way I'd imagined, the joy was still in the journey.

Mama listened intently as she combed razor-sharp parts in my hair and braided neatly positioned cornrows from front to back. When she was done, she patted the seat next to her with her hand, and I obeyed and sat down beside her. She interlocked her fingers in mine and covered the bond with her other hand. My mother's smile washed over me like I was a kid again, and just like back then, she looked straight through me, making me feel like she could read my deepest thoughts.

"Thank you for the pretty stories. I'm so proud of you," she said. "But I hear the sorrow in your voice, and God has shown me your troubles. I know you think you have it all together, and you probably do." She ran the back of her hand down the side of my cheek. "But please, take your time, just be still and listen for His voice. He'll tell you what to do," she said, her smile never leaving.

I pressed my cheek to her hand, savoring the warmth of her body touching mine. It had been years since I touched my mother. I laid my head on her shoulder, like I used to do when we sat in that pew every Sunday morning, and heeded my mama's advice—I took my time, and for the rest of our visit, we just sat still, reliving the joy of our unbroken bond.

CHAPTER 32

Their heels clicked in unison across the stone floors of Chicago's Neo-Classical City Hall building. Winston led them past the ninety-foot columns, the extravagant use of marble and the bas-relief panels depicting the principle concerns of municipal government, and out onto LaSalle Street.

"What just happened in there?" Carla said, holding her skirt against the gusts of wind whipping off of Lake Michigan.

"Complete and utter chaos," Danny said.

Winston squinted into the warm gust, "They're forcing a special election. I bet you a dozen Aldermen on that council has a candidate they want elected to that seat."

"For what benefit?" Carla asks.

Winston chuckled, "I can name a dozen off the top of my head," he said, counting them out on his hand. "To sway council votes, committee selection seats—"

"Power and greed, windy city politics," Danny said, adding to the list.

"Then we run," Carla said.

"It's not that easy. We need money for that." Danny started walking south on LaSalle toward the parking garage.

"So does everybody else," Carla said, keeping with his stride in her high heels.

"We do have a slight advantage. I started courting your name to funders when you were thinking about running before. They were on board then; no reason for them not to be now," Winston said.

"I've seen their guy. One of them, anyway," Carla said.

Winston lit a cigarette. "Enlighten us."

Carla pushed the crosswalk button. "At the developer's reception," she said, remembering literally running into Sinclair. "Young white boy."

"Someone they can easily control," Danny said.

Winston exhaled his smoke, "Developers got deep pockets. He'll be the one to beat."

The light changed and the trio dashed across the busy street. They attended the city council meeting to be present for the motion to appoint someone to Tanner's seat. Winston had entered public comments in support of the motion and introduced Daniel Boone as a viable appointee. He'd made his rounds prior to the meeting and was confident he could secure enough votes by the time council reconvened next month. Instead, one of Tanner's allies upset the plans when she put forth a motion to delay the vote.

"Alderman Tanner has not been convicted of any crimes," the ally said. "He's innocent until proven guilty. We delay the vote until after his trial. When he's found innocent, we lift the suspension, so he can get on with the business of representing the constituents of his ward."

"We can't subject those same constituents to taxation without representation while Tanner defends himself in court," an opposing Alderman shouted. "They deserve a voice on this council. I move we vote on the motion to appoint today."

The comments bounced back and forth until someone made

the case to amend the original motion to a special election based on an ordinance in the city council's charter. Once that hit the floor, the chaos erupted on the pros and cons, and by the time it was over, the motion was carried and seconded and the appointment was off the table, just like that. The council set the special election for sixty days from that day.

They headed east toward the parking garage, pushing against the strong Lake Michigan winds. Summertime in Chicago brought no relief from the winds that whipped through the tunnels formed by the downtown skyscrapers.

"We'll need a platform to run on," Carla said, pressing her skirt down from the breeze.

"It's hard to say what he'll run on, but it won't be a planning and zoning platform. No one wants to hear about their neighborhoods being gutted," Winston said. "Even though that's exactly why the developers are supporting him."

They reached the garage and Danny pushed the button for their level. "I know exactly what I'm running on," he said, holding the elevator door for his mom.

Carla stepped on the elevator ahead of the men. "What's that, son?"

"Foster Care Reform," he said as the doors closed.

Winston squashed his cigarette butt with his shoe. "That's out of left field."

"Not really. Federal prosecutor's office has a case before them that's going to blow this city's foster care system wide open. It's the perfect platform to ride into the city council," Danny said as the elevator opened.

"Enlighten me, counselor," Winston said, stepping out of the elevator and crashing into Danny, who had stopped in his tracks.

Standing in the garage was Kash, decked out in his signature

Armani suit, talking with Hunter Forsythe. "We've got sixty days, but we can make it happen. The developer's coalition will see to that," Kash said.

"That's him," Carla whispered as they walked in the opposite direction. "The young white boy the developers are pushing for Tanner's seat."

"And that Kash dude is with him," Danny said, he and Kash glanced at each other sideways. "Working with the developers and trying to strong-arm Sinclair to sell her place. I've got a bad feeling about that guy."

"You know him?" Carla asked.

"Exchanged a few words with him at Sinclair's. Some kind of wannabe developer."

Carla stopped walking. "You've been to Sinclair's?"

Danny didn't break his stride. He made it to the car and slid behind the driver's seat as Carla and Winston got in. He cranked up the engine, skidded out of the parking space and revved past Kash and Hunter.

Winston twisted to the back seat, looking at Carla, then at Danny. "What I miss?" he said, glancing back and forth between them. "Enlighten me."

CHAPTER 33

A sparrow fluttered up to my bedroom window and landed on the ledge. Her chirping drifted through the apartment announcing the beginning of another summer morning. I lay in bed listening to the songbird and remembering the hymn we sang in church so many Sundays long ago. My mother's visit, still fresh in my mind, called on me to live by her advice—just be still, and listen for His voice. The sparrow was confirmation. If his eye is on the sparrow, then I know he's keeping a close watch over me.

After my visit, I spoke with my mother's doctor; with the new medications, mama was improving. I asked if she could start week-end visits at home again like she used to do. The doctor was cautious, the lucid intervals could be temporary, and episodes could be triggered by too much stimulation, like those found outside her controlled environment. My mother had been confined for decades, but the doctor didn't recommend visits just yet.

Too much stimulation was an understatement in terms of my existence. I checked the clock by the bedside table. It was still early, but the busy day loomed ahead. In order to have any time to myself to just be still, I needed to seize the moment.

I ran a hot bath and dripped droplets of lavender oil into the water before easing into the tub and letting the oil cuddle my skin. Easing back and closing my eyes, I tried to absorb all that was happening around me. Jumping from one problem to the next gave the illusion of having it together. I was good at reciting the pretty stories, as my mother had called them, but hadn't really dealt with the situations before me. I had just pushed them aside and went on to the next thing. I was knee-deep in planning my storybook wedding and walked away from it. I'm not sure if I agree with Dr. Belo's assessment that I was afraid to get married. That somehow, my abuse was keeping me from accepting love, placing me in a constant state of anticipating doom. It was hard to convince me that I didn't walk away because Carla was all up in our business and Danny wasn't standing up to her. He was back in my life now, if only for the purpose of helping Charmaine. But he's moving forward with the run for Alderman on his own terms now with a mission to reform the foster care system, which I totally support, making our arguments about his run seem silly now. We were spending a lot of time together but hadn't given it a label. He joined Tina, Doc and me in our vigils around Jasmine and had pulled strings to get Charmaine out of juvenile detention. Vicki Summers was reassigned as her caseworker, and we were meeting today to pick up Charmaine and bring her home.

I climbed out of the tub and toweled off, catching my reflection in the mirror. Searching my face, I didn't see the sorrow that mama said she heard in my voice, but confusion lay in my furrowed brow. If I was honest with myself, there was uncertainty about so many things. Still, I had been moving so fast that I hadn't slowed down long enough to listen to the message behind the madness. Moving full speed ahead on autopilot toward my dreams and pushing anything out of the way that threatened them. Those very threats could be the voice of God that mama was talking about.

My visit with mama forced me to find a whole new way of looking at things, a way of finding myself in all of the noise. Danny's run for Alderman wasn't a negative that was to break us up, but a sign to slow down until we could put our arms around what the run was really all about—helping the hundreds of kids being mistreated in foster care.

Purchasing this building wasn't to displace Charmaine from the only place she ever lived, but God's way of whispering to me to give her a better place to live. Sherri's group home did have a strict policy by the state that prevented juveniles that had committed what was called violent acts from living there. The fact remained that Charmaine threw the book at the student. She could either get out and go into a group home with other so-called violent juvenile offenders or to an approved foster home. I didn't hesitate to offer up my home, and Vicki was all too eager to approve it. It would give me a chance to be still while we cared for Jasmine and waited on her recovery, and although tragic, another sign that I took as God telling me to be still.

The terry cloth robe caressed my skin and my favorite house slippers warmed my feet against the hardwood floor. In the kitchen, the teapot whistled, and the warmth from the sun through the kitchen window awakened my senses. I sat at the window drinking my tea and watching and listening to the morning unfold when the sparrow, as if she was following me, landed on the sill. Another sign, I thought, to just be still.

The sun rose higher in the sky, signaling time for the first order of the day. Feeling anew, I chose a yellow sundress and comfy espadrille wedges and headed out, walking the short distance to the restaurant where I was meeting Kash for breakfast. He was seated outside, under an umbrella, shaded from the sun and drinking a Bloody Mary.

"What's happening?" I said as he rose to greet me with a hug.

Kash held me at arms distance squinting at me through one-eye. "You, sunshine. All yellow and shit."

I twirled around, "It looked so good next to my chocolate skin; I couldn't resist."

"That's what I'm talking about," he said. "I couldn't pull it off with my pale face."

"But you look so good in green, though," I laughed, tugging the color on the green Izod three-button shirt he had on.

"The color of money, baby," he said, pulling the chair out. "It's all about that McCormick money," we said, in unison, laughing at our inside joke.

I ordered a mimosa and we scanned the menu for our breakfast selections. He sipped his Bloody Mary through a straw and absent-mindedly tapped his fingers on the table to some tune in his head. I'd come to learn a lot about him. He'd shared that his father, the preacher, was of the bootleg variety, having found religion after doing time in the penitentiary. Kash was born a week after his father got locked up. His white mother was a prostitute, and his daddy had been her pimp. "By the time the old man got out of prison, the old girl had caught a blade by a fellow prostitute and got dead," Kash had shared.

He had been taken care of by the women in the whore house until his father got out of prison. "I was four years old when he came and got me out of that joint. In exchange for keeping the place clean, we lived in the basement of a storefront church."

Apparently, Kash's daddy had the gift of gab. Word spread about his sermons and people came from all over to hear him preach; one of the people became Kash's step-mama. "She raised me like I was her own. My daddy preached till the day he died. Living the rest of his life like a good Christian man. Wouldn't have known he was an ex-pimp and convict if he didn't preach about his redemption. That's why people loved him so much. He was real. God looks after sinners and babies, he always said. That's who the Savior came to save, cause we all fallen short of the glory of God. Ain't nobody perfect; we all make mistakes."

I thought Kash was going to break out in the sermon the day he shared that with me. I did notice him getting a little teary-eyed and sensed it was more to it than just his father's memory that had him all choked up, but I didn't pry. We sat in silence after that for several minutes, both of us in our own thoughts. Like we were now until the waitress came over to take our order.

After the waitress left, Kash slipped a manila envelope across the table.

"What's this?" I asked, already suspecting what it was and the reason I wanted to see him in person this morning.

"That offer. Ten percent over asking."

I sipped my mimosa, stalling for the right words to come up and out in the right way. "About that," I said. "Charmaine's being released," I continued, leading with the good news first.

He smiled and nodded his head. "That's what's up? How'd you swing that?"

"Danny," I said.

Kash went silent again, but continued the tapping. "I saw him the other day. He tell you?"

I nodded.

"So, you supporting his run?"

"I haven't decided yet," I lied.

He tapped on the manila envelope, "Deals like this should be making the decision for you. Ain't nothing to think about, Sin," he said, leaning back and throwing his hands up. "From here, you buy the next one, then the next one, and you on your way to that

McCormick money. Forsythe and them boys going to pave the way for themselves, and you can just slide on in there with them. Them laws and zoning ordinance and shit they gonna pass will work in your favor, too."

I decided to rip the bandage off. "I'm not selling," I said, leaving it there.

Kash's eyes widened. "Come again?"

I shrugged, "Not right now. Going to rent out the units. Charmaine's getting—"

"Charmaine's not your problem! You going back on your word. That ain't cool. You said—"

"Wait a minute. I didn't give my word to any—"

"Damn near."

"This is real estate, damn near doesn't cut it. And why you so bent out of shape, what's the big deal?

"I got the deal right here," he said, banging his fist on the manila envelope. "I go back talking about, there's no deal here, fellows, that's my reputation on the line."

The waitress brought our food and I waited for her to leave. "I'm sorry. There's just so much going on," I said, talking low, hoping he'd lower his voice too. "I just need to be still, and—"

"I don't wanna hear that bullshit you talking about." Kash rose to his feet. If his looks could kill, I'd be dead right now. "You got that right, though, this is real estate and folks don't take to kindly to broken deals. Believe that!"

"There was no deal!" I shouted, as he marched down the sidewalk, leaving me sitting there in front of two pancake breakfasts trying to process what just happened. I gathered myself, paid the bill, and walked back home.

I hopped in my car and headed toward my next destination. Kash's reaction was heavy on my mind, which was racing, trying to conjure up an explanation that would cause him to act like that. Nothing I came up with made sense, so I did the next best thing and pushed it from my mind. What wasn't going to happen, was him ruining my day.

Vicki was waiting for me when I arrived at the juvenile camp. Security checked our identification, and we walked through a metal detector into this prison that the state insists on calling a camp. Camps are places where kids go to have fun in the summertime. This place was not that. Once past the metal detectors, we were buzzed through an iron door and met by another security station. An armed guard escorted us to a room with a sign that read: *outtake processing.*

Vicki removed a folder from her briefcase and handed it to the administrator behind the desk, who studied the papers in the file. "To be released today?" she asked.

"Yes, emergency court order," Vicki said.

The administrator sucked her teeth and searched through a file cabinet. Finding what she was looking for, she snatched up the phone receiver and made a call. "Detainee 032957. Court order release... Yeah, that's right... How soon... Got it?" She hung up the phone and tossed Vicki's file across the desk at her. "They at lunch. Have a seat; they'll bring her down when she's done."

I rolled my eyes. "I'm sure she won't mind missing whatever is thrown together for lunch in this place."

"It's procedure. You can have a seat over there."

I was about to say something else, but Vicki gave me a look that asked me to stand down. I sucked my teeth at the administrator and had a seat in one of the plastic chairs. The facility was at least a hundred years old. Water stains dotted the ceiling tiles and layers of paint covered the plastered walls. A window air conditioner sputtered a loud sound and dripped water into a bucket on the floor. I wondered if the children had air conditioning in their rooms or if they were forced to suffer through the humid Chicago summers. Everyone we had encountered upon entering the facility had a bad attitude and chip on their shoulder that I was willing to bet was taken out on the kids confined to that place. The longer I sat there, the more I became determined to help Danny get elected to that Alderman seat. Between the feds cracking down on the privatized prisons and the city on the Foster Care reform, something was going to change.

We sat there for over an hour before the door opened up and Charmaine walked through with one of the armed guards, her hands cuffed behind her back. I jumped up and went to her. The black eye was hard to miss.

"What happened? Who did this to you?" I asked her.

She leaned onto my shoulder and started sobbing. "I'm so glad to see you."

"I've been working to get you out of here," I said.

"What happened to her eye, and take these cuffs off her," Vicki said. "I'm with the Department of Child and Family services."

"What happened to your eye, detainee," the guard asked, eyeballing Vicki as he unlocked the cuffs.

"Nothing," Charmaine said, sniffling and glaring at him as she rubbed her wrist.

He looked at Vicki and me and shrugged. "See, nothing ever happens in this place," he said, handing Charmaine a trash bag he was carrying before pivoting and heading back out the door he came through.

The administrator processed Charmaine out, and the three of us went back through the iron door and past the metal detectors.

Once we were outside in the fresh air, Charmaine let out a blood-curdling scream as tears streamed down her face. "I thought I was going to die in there," she said. "What happens to me now?"

"You're coming home with me," I said, "That is if you want to."

Charmaine glanced between Vicki and me. "Seriously? You joking?"

I shook my head.

Vicki smiled, waving the file in the air. "Your approved new foster care home."

Charmaine practically jumped on my shoulders. She twirled around and did a somersault in the parking lot, landing on her feet with her hands in the air.

We said goodbye to Vicki and piled into my car with the trash bag from the guard.

"What's in the bag?" I asked.

Charmaine held it up, looking at the trash bag and then at me. "Everything I own in the world is in this bag," she said. "But that's today; it won't be like this forever."

"You got that right," I said.

We hit the freeway and Charmaine talked about the horrid conditions in the juvenile camp. From the fighting encouraged by the guards who placed bets on who would win to bugs found in her food. The incident that happened in school that landed her in the juvenile camp had been blown out of proportion, she said.

"I threw a wad of paper at this bully for calling me a dyke," she said. "When I told the teacher, she wouldn't listen, told me to sit down and shut up. Talking to me like I was trash or something. I lost my cool, balled up the paper I was working on and threw it. When she reported it to the principal, she lied and said I threw a book. There was nothing I could say after that. Nobody believed me."

"I'm so sorry that happened to you. We'll get you back in your old high school in the fall. Have you been able to go to classes since being in that place?" I asked.

Charmaine sucked her teeth, "Are you kidding? All we did all day, if they didn't have you in lock up for some bull crap, was watch TV and play Pac Man."

"They're required to offer classes."

"They didn't get that memo. Can we get something to eat?"

"For sure, fast food, okay for now?" I said.

"Long as it doesn't have bugs in it," she laughed.

I drove through a fast-food joint. We rode in silence as Charmaine devoured her burger like she hadn't eaten in months. I pulled into the hospital parking lot as she finished her last fry.

"Who sick," she asked.

I hadn't told her about Jasmine but managed to give her the clip note version as we headed into the hospital and up to her ICU room. Danny was on watch, and we were scheduled to meet Tina and Doc there for an update from Dr. Biswas.

Charmaine and I stood outside Jasmine's room, looking in through the glass. "Oh my God," was all she managed to say, seeing Jasmine surrounded by the blinking machines and ventilator.

We walked into the room just as Tina rounded the corner. "Sin!" she shouted. I told Charmaine to go on in as I waited for Tina by the door. As she approached, I felt something was off.

"What's up?" I said, clocking the worry on her face.

She shoved a yellowed and tattered newspaper clipping at me. "Look, look!" she shouted.

I read the headline, "*Remains Found in Cabrini Green Trash Shoot.*" I wasn't sure what I was reading, but I knew it couldn't be good looking at her red and puffy eyes. I continued to read out loud until I came to the sentence that told me all I needed to know, "*The remains were of a woman in her mid-thirties, wearing a pink sweater and grey plaid skirt...*" Tina's sobs filled the hospital room.

My heart sank, I wanted to tell her it could be a coincidence, but even I didn't believe that. I had no words to comfort her in this moment, so I just hugged her and held her in my arms as we walked into Jasmine's room and stood around her bed. Danny's eyes asked what was going on, but I was too distraught to respond. Intuitively he sensed my pain and walked over and placed his arm around me as I held onto Tina, who was sobbing out of control. Charmaine stood frozen by Jasmine's bedside, gently stroking her IV-taped hand.

There were no words for this moment, just the blinking light of the monitors, the rhythmic sounds of the ventilator, and the agonizing cries of a child who had lost her mother too soon.

CHAPTER 34

The choir voices filled the sanctuary and the congregation swayed, clapped and stomped their feet to the praise and worship that had taken over the Sunday morning service. The music changed and praise and worship dancers appeared before the alter, their flags trailing behind them, as they praised Him in dance to the melodic voice of the soloist singing, *His Eye Is On The Sparrow*.

I leaped to my feet and held my hands to the sky, singing along with the soloist. Danny stood up next to me, grabbing my uplifted hand in his, his baritone voice belting out my favorite hymn.

When the praise dance was over, the pastor stepped up to the pulpit, lifted his hands and the congregation stood on cue. With my free hand, I grabbed Tina's hand and nodded for her to take Charmaine's, just as the pastor said, let's us pray. I prayed for Jasmines full recovery, for Kash to overcome whatever he was going through, and for discernment in my relationship with Danny. I didn't know where we were going, but I was clear on who would get us there if it was meant to be.

We were seated in the fifth row on the right side of the sanctuary and I bowed my head at peace that I had finally found my way back home.

EPILOGUE

Life takes us in many directions, oftentimes leading us down paths that we never thought we'd venture. We can only choose to go willingly or with resistance, to either enjoy the journey or resent the ride. Whatever state of mind we choose will dictate how we receive the lessons we'll learn along the way. Lessons that are sprinkled along the path to shape us into who we are placed on this earth to become, and what we're here to do. I'm still on that journey of discovery, uncertain where my life with Danny will lead, or my guardianship of Charmaine, but the lessons born out of the stalled wedding plans and sidetracked real estate deals will lead me down a path of new adventures, unimagined possibilities and endless opportunities.

I don't know Jasmines fate as she lies in a coma locked in her own mind. Don't know if she hears me when I talk to her, or feels me when I rub lotion on her feet, what I do know is that I will be by her side until this journey ends for her, however God sees fit to end it. Just like I'll be there for Tina as she processes the tragedy of her mom's death and searches for answers that will take her down a path where she'll need good friends by her side. And though I haven't spoken to him since our encounter at breakfast, I still consider Kash a friend who I will welcome back into my life whenever he slays his own demons and returns.

I open myself up to be the vessel used for the creator's ultimate plan, not my own. Our job is to look after the least of these, the path life will take us down where our souls will be found.

Thank you for reading, *Finding* **SINCLAIR**.

Join our VIP readers club at www.storygoddesspublishing.com to be the first to hear about the next book in the continuing sage of the Sinclair Ellis series.